KNIGHTS OF CYNDROANIA

KNIGHTS OF CYNDROANIA

SHADOWS ARISING

NATHAN C. TUSHAR

Tate Publishing & *Enterprises*

Knights of Cyndroania
Copyright © 2011 by Nathan C. Tushar. All rights reserved.

No part of this publication may be reproduced, stored in a retrieval system or transmitted in any way by any means, electronic, mechanical, photocopy, recording or otherwise without the prior permission of the author except as provided by USA copyright law.

Scriptures taken from the *New American Bible*®, NAB®. Copyright © 1971 by Royal Publishers. Used by permission. All rights reserved.

This novel is a work of fiction. Names, descriptions, entities, and incidents included in the story are products of the author's imagination. Any resemblance to actual persons, events, and entities is entirely coincidental.

The opinions expressed by the author are not necessarily those of Tate Publishing, LLC.

Published by Tate Publishing & Enterprises, LLC
127 E. Trade Center Terrace | Mustang, Oklahoma 73064 USA
1.888.361.9473 | www.tatepublishing.com

Tate Publishing is committed to excellence in the publishing industry. The company reflects the philosophy established by the founders, based on Psalm 68:11,
"The Lord gave the word and great was the company of those who published it."

Book design copyright © 2011 by Tate Publishing, LLC. All rights reserved.
Cover design by Kristen Verser
Interior design by Lindsay B. Behrens

Published in the United States of America

ISBN: 978-1-61777-359-4
1. Fiction / Fantasy / Epic
2. Fiction / Fairy Tales, Folk Tales, Legends & Mythology
11.04.20

To my friends, family, and teachers for helping me make this adventure possible.

ACKNOWLEDGMENTS

Thanks to my mother and father for believing in me. And most importantly, thanks to Christopher Paolini for inspiring me to write and for showing me the magic of dragons, the greatest mystical creatures of all.

THE JOURNEY IS FOR YOU
by Nathan C. Tushar

For battles fought,
For the friendship we brought,
For the love and hope we pursue,
The journey is for you.
For every battle we win,
For every sin we commit,
For everything we do,
I will fight for you.
For in every soul,
There is a light.
For in every soul,
There is also darkness, and it obscures your sight.
For in every heart,
There is a power greater than any one thing.
For in every great journey,
There is also a great story.
For every sunrise,
There is a beauty like no other.
For every sunset,
There is always sadness.
For the ones we love,
We fight for their freedom,
For the ones we dread,
We fight them to see another day.
For every living thing,
For everyone's freedom,
I march on to fight for you,
And the journey is for you.

PROLOGUE:
NIGHT OF SORROW
EIGHTEEN YEARS EARLIER

The wind howled through the breathless night, sending a deathly chill down the soldier's spine. The wind started getting cold. The only things that could be heard were clanking footsteps in the distance and the crackling flames of the torches on the walls. The sounds seemed to grow louder, and the air grew colder. Fear gripped the soldier, freezing him in place. The dancing flames from the torches started to go out, one by one, leaving the outpost in darkness. The only light was from the dimly lit moon. Moving his hand, the soldier signaled the archers to stand ready.

"The Shadow Lord is here. Now is not the time to be afraid. Tonight we fight to defend our kingdom!" the soldier yelled to his men. "Now draw your swords and show this man who and what we are! Give our king the time he needs. *Charge!*"

The men drew their swords, charging at their ancient enemy, roaring deathly war cries.

A warrior on dragon-back stopped and looked behind him at his kingdom. The sound of charging soldiers came from the south entrance. "It's started," said the warrior. "We have to hurry now, Legacy. I need you to run faster than the wind, girl."

"You can count on that, Koichi," said Legacy. "And I'll try not to wake the youngling."

In Koichi's arms was a sleeping baby wrapped in a white cloth. "He's the only son I have now, and I'm never going to let anything happen to him. Let's get going, shall we?"

Legacy started to turn back to the forest and said, "Do you really believe that?" Then she stood on her hind legs and roared loudly. Suddenly, an explosion shattered the cold night. They wheeled around and saw a ball of fire in the center of the city, followed by a powerful shockwave.

"No!" Koichi watched as the ball of fire got bigger, and then yelled, "Run, Legacy! Run!"

Legacy wheeled back around with a jolt and darted into the night. *We need to fly Legacy! Take off in that clearing ahead. These trees are slowing us down!* With a nod, Legacy sped up. When they reached the clearing, Legacy snapped her wings open, and with one powerful downwards stroke, she launched off the ground and into the night. As they flew above the forest, the ball of fire grew bigger and bigger. The fireball destroyed everything in its path, only to stop at the forest's end. As soon as the treetops were behind them, Legacy dove to the ground and landed with a thud. She turned to look at the once beautiful forest. All that remained were ashes.

"Why?" Koichi wept, tears trickling down his face. He shuddered and then lifted his head to the heavens and howled into the night, "*Why?*"

"Koichi," said Legacy, "there's nothing we can do now. We must reach Master Voggna's temple. If we don't make it there, your—" she eyed the baby then continued,—"son will have no future! Is that what you want?"

"No," said Koichi with a lump in his throat. "No. I don't want that. Let's get to Master Voggna's. We need to go through the Draggonian Forest to get there."

"I know the way," said Legacy with a scowl. "You act like I don't know anything." Then she took off into the night sky once more.

To Koichi's surprise, the baby didn't wake from the explosion. They went on for several hours, traveling across Spirit Field to the Draggonian Forest. As they flew over the Draggonian Forest, a wolf howled in the distance. It was close. "We can't stop now, Legacy. We're almost there!" Koichi said.

"Agreed," Legacy acknowledged. The wolf howled again. This time it was directly in front of them.

Koichi started to panic. "We're not going to make it!"

Suddenly, a wolf black as the night leapt up from the forest below and hovered in the air in front of them. Then the air around it swirled with black smoke blocking the wolf from view. When the smoke began to clear, a black dragon emerged. Without warning, the dragon rammed Legacy in the chest, forcing her backwards. "Run, Master

Koichi! Run!" yelled Legacy, tearing and slashing at the black dragon. "Go on without me!"

With supernatural speed, Koichi ran up Legacy's neck and leapt off her muzzle. Holding the baby even tighter, he fell in between the trees with a rough landing, then ran through the night. He drew his sword, and his speed increased with every step.

Where did Fenrir come from? he asked himself. *And how did he find us? What ever the reason, there's no stopping now. I must get to the temple.*

As Voggna's temple came into view, the light from the gem in his amulet vanished and then shattered. A horrifying roar echoed throughout the forest, and a loud thud came soon after it with an ear-piercing screech, and then there was silence.

"Legacy, no!" He ran to the temple doors, trying to hold back his sorrow for his loss. Once inside, he slammed the doors behind him and bolted it shut. He ran through the temple garden in the direction of the room he once stayed in while living there. He placed the baby on the bed, slouched into a nearby chair, and wept, no longer able to hold back his tears. Then he cried out to the night, "Why? Why did they have to die? First Emily and now Legacy! They didn't deserve this!"

Weeping, he placed his golden sword next to the baby, along with a black sword from his other sheath. Then he placed a letter on both of the swords that read:

Master Voggna, as you feared, my kingdom has fallen to the Shadow Lords. The baby before you is my son, Ryuu, but I've given him the name Cyno, after my brother-in-law's middle name; he will hopefully be looking in soon. He will come as a silver wolf. Next to him is his sword and mine. They're the only gifts I can give him. Give them to him when the time is right. When he knows his destiny. Take care of him for me. My time draws near to its end. Keep him safe. Teach him the ways of the Dragon Knights. Give him a better future. A future where darkness doesn't dwell."

Your old friend,
Koichi Dragonfang

With that, he left the room and was never heard from again.

PRINCE RYUU'S DREAM

"We fight as one! For Cyndroania, for Riverside, for the fallen kingdom, for my father! Charge!" Prince Ryuu yelled.

"You think you can stop me, you fools?" Lord Mávro Dráko asked, saying it as if he were invincible.

"Be careful, my knights, and good luck!" said Lady Arabella, hoping that the new Dragon Knights would bring peace again.

"We will, m'lady. We won't let you down!" said Sir Kouri, who then called for his dragon, Arctic.

"Aluxio!" called Prince Ryuu to his dragon.

"Leanna, we need to protect Cyndroania!" said Princess Elizabeth.

"Aeolus, let's blow the enemy away!" said Prince Aquilo.

"Rah, Iffiris! Let's turn up the heat, boy!" bellowed Prince Conlaodh with great strength.

"Crayoatha, let's go, boy!" said Malak the Draggonian.

As the heroes of Cyndroania charged forward toward the army of living shadows that Lord Mávro Dráko conjured,

Prince Ryuu noticed he did not order his army to attack at all but instead just stood there, motionless. What was he up to? But then he realized it. He saw what was coming from the east. It was Mávro Dráko's dragon! And before he could warn Elizabeth, Mávro Dráko's dragon rammed right into her and Leanna! Prince Ryuu yelled, "Elizabeth, no!"

Elizabeth fell to the ground unhurt, but Leanna was wounded badly and fell with a big thud that shook the earth. "Lean—"

Mávro Dráko's dragon pinned both Leanna and Elizabeth to the ground with his massive claws. Elizabeth screamed.

"So now you will witness the full power of my dragon!" said Lord Mávro Dráko.

The dragon was enormous. Its wings were ablaze with black and purple flames; its head was made of shadows; its eyes burned crimson red; its roar pierced Ryuu to the bone. The dragon was half flesh, half shadow. To Ryuu's horror, the dragon shot black shadowy flames from its maw at Elizabeth, engulfing her in shadows.

Ryuu woke in horror, screaming at the top of his lungs, "Elizabeth!"

"What's all the racket?" said a voice from the doorway.

"Sorry, Master Voggna, I didn't mean—"

"It's the dreams again, isn't it, Ryuu?"

"Yes, Master, it is. Oh, but what does it mean? It makes no sense! I'm only seventeen for crying out loud! When the heck are you going to tell me what they mean? Well?" he asked his master with so much anger that the scar on his wrist began to burn. "And the scar on my wrist, you never tell me a—"

"That's enough Cyno. You're old enough now, and it's about time I tell you," said Voggna, calmly.

"You haven't called me Cyno in a long time," said Ryuu, looking down at his bed sheets.

"I know, Ryuu, but that's also what your father wanted you to be named. The day he left you in my care, about eighteen years ago, I never got the chance to see him. He left in such a hurry. Now, get dressed, and come to my room."

Ryuu nodded; Voggna left him to get dressed. Ryuu did not move for a while for his scar was still burning. He looked at it for another minute, wondering where he got it in the first place. He had it as long as he can remember. He sighed then got dressed.

It was nearly morning when Ryuu left his room. He took a stroll through the flower gardens and then he headed toward Voggna's room. When he got there, he looked at his wrist. He was finally going to know the answers to his dreams and how he got his scar. He knocked on the door, then opened it and entered the room. He had never seen his master's room before. It was more of a study compared to his room. It was filled with books on dragons, armor, magic, magical forgery, magical elements, and swordplay. And there on the wall behind Voggna's desk was a sword made of gold with a pledge underneath it that read, "I am the Sword of Light, Destiny. The Sword of Koichi, the first Dragon Knight." Ryuu stared at it for a moment. Then he realized that his master was at his desk looking at him with knowing eyes, being patient.

"Come, Ryuu. It's time I told you what you are."

THE HISTORY OF DRAGON KNIGHTS

Ryuu sat down in a chair in front of the desk.

"I know you've been waiting a long time for this, Ryuu," said his master. "Ryuu, you have the blood of a Dragon Knight. You have the markings—your scar on your wrist for instance."

Ryuu glanced at his scarred wrist and then looked back up at his master. "And what about the dreams, Master?" he asked.

"They're not dreams, Ryuu. They are visions."

Ryuu's eyebrows rose with wonder and excitement. "The visions are showing the coming future. Your future!" Ryuu could not believe what he was hearing. After waiting for five years, he finally knew what his purpose in life was.

"Ryuu, I want you to have this." From within his robe pocket, Voggna gave him a necklace with a golden dragon holding a tourmaline crystal between its wings. Ryuu looked at it with awe.

"What is this?" he asked.

"It is a Draggonian necklace," said Voggna. "Once you put it on, there's no turning back."

Ryuu hesitated for a bit, and then he put it on. His scar burned. The blood rushed from his head, and he collapsed to the floor. As his vision blurred and his eyes started to close, he was in the middle of a battlefield. Two dragons battled inside a ring of flames.

Ryuu could not believe his eyes. He was looking at the final battle of the very first Shadow War. He was looking at Koichi and some strange black hooded figure in armor like none other. The armor was black and crimson with an evil eye upon its chest plate. The armor was shaped like a dragon's body. Its shoulders were small wings; the metal plating was shaped like scales; the hand guards and the boots were shaped like the dragon's claws. Koichi's armor was the same, but black and gold like his dragon.

The black hooded stranger spoke. "You think you can stop me, brother? I'm more powerful than you and more powerful than any one! I have killed many of your knights, but you still remain. Now I shall crush you!"

"You're a fool, Tarin!" bellowed Koichi, "You and your dragon are no match for me and my own! Legacy!" His dragon attacked, driving its huge, sharp fangs into the other dragon's neck.

"Deception!" yelled Tarin as his dragon roared with agony. Tarin's eyes burned crimson. He wanted to have blood shed around him, not his dragon's, but everyone else's blood, especially Koichi's blood. Koichi's dragon, Legacy, was still holding on to Deception's neck, still roaring with pain.

"No! Make it stop, make it stop!" screamed Ryuu, lying on the floor, his eyes closed tight, tears coming out from underneath his eyelids, sweat pouring down his face. His hands were holding his head as if it were going to explode. His master just stood there, watching with sympathy.

As the vision continued, Koichi and Tarin fought for hours, never letting the other get an advantage over the other.

"Enough!" yelled Koichi, swinging his sword at his brother. Their blades met, but Koichi swung so fast and hard, he knocked Tarin back, making him soar two feet above the ground, a hundred yards away, knocking Tarin's sword out of his hand. Koichi caught the blade. He started to hover above the ground and began to glow bright yellow. His cape rose in the air; the blades started to float in midair by his hands. He moved his hands closer together, and the swords moved with them. With a ray of light, the two swords joined together, creating a single blade of light and darkness.

"Now we end this! Once and for all! Legacy!" he bellowed, calling his dragon. Legacy threw Deception aside and then joined her master again. She jumped high in the air, spreading her massive wings, and then turned into a glowing ball of light and zoomed toward the blade, combining her strength with it. The blade started to glow, and Koichi sped toward Tarin with such speed he left a ghostly image of himself behind. Tarin staggered upright, but before he could move to avoid the blow, the blade drove right through his heart. He gasped, coughing up blood.

"No more! It's over—you, your dragon, and your reign of terror!" said Koichi. His voice echoed with great power.

Tarin suddenly laughed, spewing blood on Koichi's face. Then he smirked, "Oh no, not yet, Dragon Knight. You may have won this war, but I will triumph in the end. I shall return, and so will my dragon."

"Really? Well I don't think so! I expected more, Tarin!" Putting his foot on Tarin's chest, right below where the blade was, Koichi pushed off, jumping off of Tarin, pulling the sword out of his chest, making a one-eighty, and landing facing the opposite direction, kneeling, holding the sword in the air off to his side and the other arm to his chest.

Tarin was motionless, a smirk still on his face. His eyes were still and empty; he collapsed to the ground. Deception lay motionless, dead as well. The ring of fire was no more; the sky lit up again. The sun started to shine. The war was over. Then a roar of cheers started to echo across the land. Then Koichi held the sword up high, and the sun reflected off its blade. Then a roar of a dragon joined in on the cheering with the sound of victory!

Then the vision was over.

Ryuu got up. His head was pounding, his whole body was trembling, and his scar still burned. With the help of his master, he sat back down in the chair. Ryuu looked down at his lap, trying to ease the pain in his throbbing head, panting very hard.

"Ryuu, do you feel all right to talk?" asked his master.

"I...I think so," he answered.

"Then tell me what you saw in the vision." Ryuu hesitated for a while, trying to catch his breath, and then spoke. For three long hours, he spoke to his master, telling him everything he saw in the vision. After he finished speaking, he looked up. The sun was shining bright in the window. Then he looked at the golden sword he had seen in the vision. He looked to the left of it. A sword with a black blade was right next to it. How had he not noticed it before? It also had a pledge under it that read: The Blade of Darkness, Blood Fang

"Master Voggna, isn't that the same sword that..." He paused, trying to remember the name. "Master, isn't that the same sword that Tarin used?" He pointed to the wall, indicating the black one.

Voggna turned around in his chair and, "My dear boy, that is the very same. That sword protected and slaughtered many people and dragons." When he finished, tears fell from his eyes.

"What do you mean, Master?" asked Ryuu.

Tears fell from Voggna's eyes, and then he said, "I'm not sure if I should tell you yet, Ryuu. The information may discomfort you. There's a reason why I don't talk about it very often."

"Still, Master," said Ryuu, "I want to know."

Voggna hesitated for a moment and then gave in. "Very well. I'll tell you, but understand that I'm only telling you what I know." Ryuu nodded. "Good. Now I believe I'll start from the beginning.

"Many years ago, before you were born, the land had once had many Dragon Knights. They protected the land and sky, never letting evil rule over them. Your father and his brother were the first two Dragon Knights of Cyndroania, exactly two millenniums ago."

Ryuu jumped in his chair. "Two millenniums ago! But that's impossible. I would already be dead!"

Voggna raised an eyebrow. "Long ago, yes. Impossible, no. You see, a Dragon Knight could live for a very long time. Depending on what age they were when they touched their dragon for the very first time, they would look exactly the same forty or more years later. They grew old, yes, but their lives were extended. The only way for them to die was to die in combat. A fatal blow from a sword or an arrow could kill them. Another way was to poison them or using a death spell. The option of using a death spell took so much time, very few died by that method."

Ryuu pondered what his master said and then asked, "So if Koichi and Tarin were born over two thousand years ago, they would still look the same today?" He thought that was absurd. Surely it must have happened only twenty or so years ago. *But if it did happen that long ago, my father and uncle must have been ancient,* he thought to himself with disbelief.

KNIGHTS OF CYNDROANIA

"Yes, they would, Ryuu. Time never ravaged them. They were very old, yes, but strong and powerful. They each had the strength of twelve men, but over the years, they became a two-man army and were never defeated! But as more years passed, Tarin wanted all the power for himself and betrayed his kind and attacked Koichi. Koichi had the upper hand though. It was a thousand to one. With the help of so many Dragon Knights at Koichi's side, Tarin slew his apprentice and fled, leaving everything in flames. He was never heard from for over five hundred years. When he returned, he was no longer a Dragon Knight. He was a Shadow Lord. He came back with an army of living shadows." Voggna paused; another tear ran down his face. "This army was so powerful that it nearly destroyed all of Cyndroania. Everything was in chaos. Those days were the darkest times of our land."

"That was the beginning of the Shadow Age, wasn't it, Master?" Ryuu asked.

"Very good, my Prince. Very good. The Shadow Age was, as you may know, full of evil. Unknown beings and shadow creatures roamed the land killing many. Also during this age, Tarin killed every single Dragon Knight one by one, all except for Koichi. When that battle came, many people regained their lost hope. As you know, Koichi won in the end. Eighteen years ago, Tarin did return, not to destroy, but to protect you, his family, and the Garindel Kingdom, which was destroyed, but not by his hands."

"What?" gasped Ryuu. "Why would he want to do that?"

"Because," said Voggna, "from what I am told, he was innocent. He came to me the same night you were brought here by Koichi. He told me where he was during all those years of darkness. He said that he was looking for answers to why all the terror was happening again."

"Hang on!" interrupted Ryuu, "If he didn't destroy the Garindel Kingdom, who did?"

"From what Tarin told me, it was someone who's supposed to be dead."

"But why did he have a change of heart?"

"Ah," said Voggna, "that, I don't know. But when he learned what was causing the chaos across Cyndroania, he fled in fear. Even after so many years have passed, he is still terrified of the thing that turned him evil when he was very young."

"What was that?"

"The same thing that's supposed to be dead."

"So after that, my father left me here in your care that night, right?" asked Ryuu, just to reassure himself.

"Exactly, Ryuu, exactly. Now the books on these shelves are yours to read. Learn as much as you can. The information in them is all about Dragon Knight law." Rising from his chair, Voggna said, "Now if you'll excuse me, I must attend to other matters. Have fun reading about Dragon Knights, Ryuu."

Before Voggna left the room, Ryuu said, "Master?"

Voggna stopped and turned to face him. "Yes?"

Ryuu thought for a second and then said, "Master, something doesn't add up."

Voggna raised an eyebrow. "And what is that, Ryuu?"

"Wasn't Tarin killed when Koichi stabbed him?"

Voggna stared at him in the doorway. "Tarin didn't die."

"But then who did die?"

Voggna sighed. "That is the greatest mystery today. Who was that man that Koichi killed those many years ago?" And with that, he left the room.

THE ELEVEN DRAGON EGGS AND INVITATION

It had been three days since Ryuu learned about the Dragon Knights, and the sun shone brightly in the sky. Ryuu was in his bedroom reading books from Voggna's study. He had almost read half the books from his master's room. He enjoyed the books; the servants had to bring him his food because he refused to leave his room. The books were piled up to the ceiling. Ryuu would ask his master questions every once and a while on some subjects, like how the forgery of a sword with one or more of the eight magical elements worked. The eight elements were fire, nature, light, energy, darkness, wind, water, and ice. He was about to read the next book on the pile when a servant came in and said, "Master Ryuu, Master Voggna wants to speak with you."

"Can it wait? I was about to start another book. You know what? Never mind. I'm coming. Tell him I'll be right there."

The servant replied, "Yes, Master Ryuu, it will be done." Then he left the room. Ryuu put his book aside and went to his master's loft. When he entered the room, there were eleven large eggs on a table, nicely preserved. From their size and shape, Ryuu could tell that they were dragon eggs. He looked for his master, but he wasn't there. So he decided to enter and wait for him. Heading over to the dragon eggs, he started to examine them.

"Dragon eggs. Fascinating things, aren't they?"

Ryuu jumped at the sound of his master's voice. He had forgotten about why he was there. He turned around to see his master in the doorway and asked, "Master, these are dragon eggs?"

Then his master replied, "Yes, they are, and they are yours to watch over, for this is your first task, Cyno. These dragon eggs belong to their very own chosen one. I want you to find the other eight chosen ones."

Ryuu was confused. *There are eleven eggs there, but I'm supposed to find only eight chosen ones. One of the eggs is probably mine, so that means there's ten eggs left with only eight to be given to their chosen owners, ruling out two from the remaining ten eggs. What could be wrong with the remaining two eggs that I shouldn't find their chosen ones?*

"Master, which eggs are not to be brought to their chosen ones?" he asked. "Are they the indigo egg and the coral red one?"

His master hesitated for a moment and then said, "Yes. Those are the ones that you don't have to worry about. But this one"—he was indicating the black, gold, and silver dragon egg on the table—"is your egg. Go ahead and take a closer at it."

As Ryuu looked closer at the egg, he noticed that there was a strange dragon symbol on it. The symbol resembled a dragon's head that had six horns: four going back, the other two curved forward down the muzzle. It was exactly the same as the one on his wrist.

They sat in silence for several minutes. During that time, Ryuu wondered what element the three strange dragon eggs were. *Maybe they're light and nature, but that wouldn't make any sense. Or maybe light and darkness. Or maybe they're entirely new elements. Whatever they are, I've never seen dragon eggs like these three.*

"Master," he said, "can you tell me the history of these three eggs?"

Voggna grimaced. "I would tell you, but the only thing I know is that they're Legacy's and Deception's eggs."

Ryuu jumped in his chair. "They mated? But I thought they hated each other!"

Voggna raised an eyebrow. "You're forgetting about their history before that. When they were younger, they fell deeply in love with each other. Five hundred years before the Shadow Wars, the two of them mated. Out of their twelve eggs, these three were the last. Koichi must have known what the eggs' purposes were because three nights after Legacy laid her eggs, he took them away from the nest. Legacy knew, of course, because he told her of his plan. They could feel the darkness rising in Tarin. Five weeks later, Tarin betrayed them, but in those five weeks, Koichi put a spell on the eggs to give them protection and gave them to a man named Christopher who forged three swords of a great power. He did this in the forgotten Tower of Cyndrio, also known as the Tower of Twilight. When he was finally finished making the swords, he stabbed them into a stone dais and left the eggs at the base of a dragon statue and then left Cyndrio Tower forever." Ryuu looked down at his lap, pondering what he had learned.

*Later that day, Ryuu went over to the stables to see the horses. When he entered the stable, a row of ten horses ran down on each side. One of the ten stood out, his horse, Winter. When she saw him, she whinnied and tossed her mane. When Ryuu took her out of her stall, he noticed that her lips seemed to be curled into a little smile. He chuckled at the sight of it. Guiding her to the grooming tools, he grabbed a brush and softly stroked it across her back. After he was done checking for mats and dirt on her back, he grabbed Winter's saddle and blanket and put them on her.

"All right, you ready to have a little fun, Winter?" he said to her playfully. She whinnied happily. Climbing onto her back, Ryuu guided her outside.

"Ah, Master Ryuu, are you going out onto the fields?" asked one of the servant.

"Yes, I am. Can you tell Master Voggna that I'm leaving for a while?" The servant nodded and then left him to see Voggna.

*As they trotted along the road to the fields, Ryuu listened to the sounds of the forest. He heard a creek off in the distance, the birds in the trees above, the wind calmly rustling through the leaves, and the soft singing of fairies in the distance. Suddenly, something ran in front of them, making Winter rear.

Holding on for dear life, Ryuu tried to calm her down. "Whoa there! Easy, Winter!" When she finally calmed down, he patted her gently on her neck. "Come on now. Whatever it was, it's not going to hurt you."

He looked around, trying to see if he could spot the thing that nearly made him fall off his horse. There was nothing in sight, and the curiosity to know what it was faded from his mind. Eventually, they reached the fields. It was a beautiful sight. Flowers were everywhere, from day lilies to morning glories to birds of paradise to Ryuu's favorite, the dragon's heart. The dragon's heart was given its name for its crimson flower. Its leaves were in the shapes of hearts, and its thorns that ran down only one side in a straight line. Like the morning glory, it opened at midmorning and withered by midday. Ryuu took a deep breath, hypnotized by their beautiful smells.

When the sun got low, Ryuu guided Winter back to the forest. As they went back, he saw little flower fairies glowing in the forest. It was much darker in there now. At the mouth of the forest path, three of them were waiting for him. Trying to remember their speech, Ryuu said, "*Elet, wiltree eo mera tria kaj mari ya healse?* (Hello, friends. Will you help me find my way back?) The fairy in the middle nodded and said, "*Moran.*" (Come, and follow.) And the three of them flittered away.

As Ryuu followed, he asked them in their tongue, "Did you see anything unusual in the forest today?"

The same fairy that answered him earlier spoke in his musical voice. "No, I didn't. Why do you ask, Prince Ryuu?"

He just shrugged and said, "Well, something fast went by earlier in front of my horse. She almost threw me off when she reared in fright."

The fairy shrugged. "I don't know what you're talking about. It must have been a new creature of the forest."

For a time, they were silent until one of the fairies said, "*Meeroadoe! Meeroadoe!*"

"What's he saying?" asked Ryuu.

"The temple is just up ahead. Go now. Your master awaits you." The fairies then flew away in the almost twilight-covered forest.

When Ryuu got inside the temple, a servant ran up to him. "Master Ryuu, Master Voggna would like to see you immediately. Hurry! Time is running out!"

Ryuu jumped off Winter's back fearing the worst. "Take care of her for me please. Make sure she gets a good rest."

With that, he sped off to Voggna's study leaving the servant behind, who hollered, "Yes, Master Ryuu, but I don't think she's going to get to rest for too long. You'll be needing her again soon!"

Passing many servants, Ryuu entered Voggna's study. "Master Voggna, you called for me?" he said, bending over trying to catch his breath.

Voggna raised an eyebrow and said, "You came here in a hurry." When Ryuu looked up, there was another man in the room wearing a black cloak. In his hand was a letter.

The man in the black cloak turned to Ryuu and said, "This letter is addressed to you. You have been invited to the Riverside Kingdom Festivities by their king." The man handed Ryuu the letter. Taking it, Ryuu started to open the letter. The man walked past him towards the door and said, "It's good to see you alive again, Cyndrio". Startled, Ryuu found himself nodding. He turned around to look at the man, but he was already gone.

"What was that about?" he asked.

Voggna just shrugged and said, "I don't know." Ryuu cocked an eyebrow, not believing him. "I'm telling you, Ryuu. I really don't know. He must have mistaken you for someone else, but in any case, you need to prepare for your journey."

Ryuu nodded. "All right, I'll get dressed and then leave immediately." And with that, he left the room to prepare for traveling.

TO RIVERSIDE

Ryuu's servants prepared a wonderful garment for him. It was a very dark, almost black, sapphire robe. There were patches of scale-like armor around the chest and shoulders. There was also a black leather belt with a beautiful sapphire gem surrounded by silver on the buckle. A little pouch hung from one side. A cape, the same color as the robe, hung from the neck from a silver chain. Ryuu couldn't believe his eyes.

"Master! Where did you get this? And how could you afford such beautiful clothes?" he asked with amazement.

Then Master Voggna replied, "Why, they're yours. Your parents gave them to you in their will, which is just some of the things they owned. All those things are yours now. Oh, I almost forgot. I also want you to have this. The young man that came by earlier left this for you." He handed Ryuu an amethyst-colored blade with a silver hilt, and a dragon headed cross guard along with a silver sheath.

"Thank you, Master Voggna. How will I ever repay you?"

"You can't," chuckled Voggna. "Now get going, or you'll be late for the opening feast up at the castle." Ryuu nodded, then got in his robes and called for his horse and set off. He followed the path through the forest at a swift pace, trying to make it to Riverside before the opening feast started. Ryuu came to a halt at the mouth of the entrance to the forest and saw a beautiful castle in the distance over the trees. "That must be the place," he said. "We're almost there, Winter. Once we're there, you can take a nice long rest, okay girl?"

Winter whinnied in approval and then Ryuu urged her forward toward the castle. As they galloped through the clearing of Spirit Field, the sun was just barely visible over the tops of the trees. Ryuu and Winter galloped through Forest Evergreen. There were signs posted for travelers to tell them which path to take to the castle.

Nightfall came as they followed the path to the city gates; he saw a wolf following them. It wasn't an ordinary wolf from what he could tell. Its fur coat shone silver in the moonlight. There were also strange symbols on it that ran from head to tail, the same symbols on his dragon egg. The same symbols were on its shoulders as well. Trying to ignore it, Ryuu rode on. When the city entrance came into view, the gates were starting to close. Panicking, Ryuu signaled to the guards to wait while making Winter go into a sprint. The gate was almost halfway closed. Ducking his head, he and Winter barely made it in.

"You cut that pretty darn close," said one of the guards. "Sorry about that, but the gate has to close by this time of night, mostly to keep out wild animals. So who's your wolf friend there? I've never seen one like him."

"What?" said Ryuu, and he turned around. To his surprise, he saw the same wolf that had followed him. It sat there panting, a smile on its face and wagging its tail happily. Turning back to the guard, he said, "I don't really know. He followed me here actually."

The guard chuckled. "Well, that's something. It must be fond of you or something."

The wolf barked in agreement. Ryuu turned to look at it again and then said, "Anyway, I'm probably late for the party. Do I take this road all the way to the castle?"

The guard nodded. "Just follow the road, and it will lead you right to the castle's front gate. If you hurry, you might make it there before they start the feast."

Ryuu turned and had Winter gallop down the road through the city.

*By the time Ryuu got to the castle, the party had already started. "Great!" he said to himself. "I'm late. Well, as I promised, you can have a nice long rest, okay, Winter?" The two of them started to trot slowly to the main gate.

"Invitation plea—," requested one of the guards, stopping midsentence when he saw him. Ryuu reached into his bag, pulling out the invitation, and handed it to the guard. The guard accepted it and then started to read it. He looked at it for a couple of minutes and then asked,

"Are you"—he looked back at the invitation to make sure of himself—"Prince Ryuu, sir?"

"Yes, I am," Ryuu replied.

The guard glared at him with anger in his eyes, "Why aren't you dead like your cursed father?"

"What?" *What is he talking about? My father was a good man.* "Look, I'm not lying," Ryuu went on, not really knowing what to say. "I've traveled from the very center of the Draggonian Forest and across Spirit Field to get here. Listen, my horse is very ti—"

"You may come in," said a voice. "Guards, take his horse to the royal stables, understood?" Ryuu got off Winter and saw a tall man wearing a crown on his head. The man walked toward him. Ryuu bowed. "Ryuu, welcome to my castle. I've been expecting you for some time," said the man.

"How do you know my name?" asked Ryuu.

The man replied, "Well, I have known you ever since you were a baby. Yes, I knew your parents, Ryuu, and I sent the invitation." Ryuu stood there in shock. He never expected to meet someone that knew him.

So he's known me since I was a baby. He might know something about my past. Maybe he could tell me which kingdom I am really from. "Are we related?" asked Ryuu.

The man chuckled. "No, my dear boy. We're not related. I am one of your father's friends, and he made me one of your guardians."

Ryuu went on asking questions, trying not to sound surprised. "Do you know which kingdom I'm from?"

"We Drag—I mean, well, you see," the man stuttered, "your kingdom, Ryuu, has fallen to the Dark Moon." He stopped and then looked at the ground.

"The what?" asked Ryuu. "What's the Dark Moon?"

The man replied, "An evil, terrifying beast of darkness known as Fenrir! But let's not talk about that right now. Let me introduce you to the guests, and then I'll introduce you to my family. Please, come with me. The feast is about to begin. They're expecting us."

A FEAST OF ROYALTY

After going though many corridors, Ryuu and the king arrived at the ballroom. There were thousands of people around long tables lined up in the center of the hall. Minstrels played on a stage at the far side of the room. People surrounded them, listening to their favorite melodies. The room was decorated with silky curtains around the archways. Flowers were placed around in every corner of the room, and the outside balcony had a great view of the moonlit sky.

"Are the decorations to your liking?" the king asked him.

"Yes," he replied. "They're very beautiful."

"Good to know," said the king. "I'll introduce you to the guests now." With a snap, two guards blew their trumpets to announce the new arrival. Everything went silent as all eyes fixed on the two of them. The king walked forward and bellowed to his guests, "Attention, everyone! I want each and every one of you to give our most important guest a warm welcome. He is the last of the fallen kingdom's royal family. I introduce to you Prince Ryuu!"

With a thunderous roar, people started to clap their hands together, welcoming him to the festivities. Some glared. Ryuu had a suspicious feeling that they, like the guard he met earlier, believed that his father was a traitor. As the king and Ryuu walked through the excited crowd of people, they finally made it to the far end of the table. The king slouched into his chair, exhausted. Ryuu took a seat to the king's right. To the king's left sat four women, each of them were wearing a crown.

"Ryuu, I'd like you to meet my family. This is my wife, Elaine." He gestured to the tall woman. Ryuu bowed. Then the king gestured to the three girls. "My youngest daughter, Cassea; my second daughter, Melanie; and my firstborn, Elizabeth."

Looking at the girls, Ryuu noticed how beautiful their dresses were. Cassea was wearing a blue dress made of silk. He looked at Melanie; she was wearing a beautiful sapphire blue dress with silver stars stitched around the edges of her sleeves and around the bottom of the dress. He then eyed Elizabeth. She was wearing a white dress with a teal trim around the sleeves and the bottom of the dress had stars like Melanie's. Then, Ryuu began to notice that he could smell a different fragrant around the three princesses. Cassea smelled like sweet strawberries that had been sliced open. Melanie smelled like fresh oranges, and Elizabeth had the smell of white peonies that had just blossomed. The next thing Ryuu noticed was their hair. Cassea had long honey-blonde hair like her mother, Elaine. Melanie had brown hair that went down to her shoulders. And Elizabeth had golden brown hair that was long and cascaded down her back, waving in the wind. Ryuu then noticed how their ages differed. Cassea looked to be around ten years old. Melanie was at least thirteen to fourteen years old. Elizabeth looked to be about his age.

Consumed by their beauty, Ryuu introduced himself. "I'm Prince Ryuu, as you know. It is an honor to meet you, all of you." He then bowed his head to them. Then it occurred to him that the king never introduced himself. Turning around, he said, "My lord, you never told me your name."

The king cursed at himself through clenched teeth then said, "Dragon scales, that's right! I beg your pardon. My name is King Abrithil of Riverside. Well, let's enjoy the party, Ryuu. You can even dance with my daughters after the tournaments if you like."

Blushing, Ryuu said, "Thank you. I'll consider your offer, and what tournaments?"

"The festival of course. We will be traveling to a town called Lakeside tomorrow to begin the celebrations. You see, every year on my birthday, we host many games through the course of many days to complete each competition. The games mainly consist of an archery contest, a jousting tournament, and other things."

"Sounds like a lot of fun."

Abrithil chuckled and then rose from his chair, and all heads turned toward him. "Before we start the feast,

I would like everyone to put their hands together in prayer." Everyone did as the king asked.

Then all at once, they chanted: "Father, hallowed be your name, your kingdom come. Give us each day our daily bread. Forgive us our sins, for we too forgive all who do us wrong; and subject us not to the trial." Then the king added, "In the life of the faithful, the aim of all that we have said up to now is the final reckoning that the faithful be really nourished and live from the written Word of God. Amen."

"Amen," the guests echoed. Then Abrithil announced with a cheery voice, "Let the feast begin!"

At once, people resumed their conversations as the food was brought out by the servants. Ryuu gazed at all of the different foods that were laid out on the tables. There was roasted boar, goose, beef, and chicken. There were baskets full of freshly baked bread, boats of gravy, bowls full of roasted potatoes and carrots, jars filled with the finest wines, plates of a variety of different cheeses, and a giant platter of meat in the center of the table that Ryuu didn't recognize.

"What is this?" he asked Abrithil. "I've never seen this kind of meat before."

Abrithil chuckled. "That is dragon meat, Ryuu. It is the rarest meat there is because people don't hunt dragons. The dragons don't mind that we take their dead. Most of the time dragons leave their dead to rot and decay. One large dead dragon can feed about a quarter of the guests here tonight. We only serve it on important birthdays."

"Is it your birthday, m'lord?" asked Ryuu.

Abrithil chuckled again, taking a bite of dragon meat. "Well, it's both of ours. You turn eighteen tomorrow, and I turn fifty-two the day after. Oh, and they added a pinch of mint. They've outdone themselves again, my dearest."

Elaine laughed. "You say that every year."

"But it's true!" retorted Abrithil.

Ryuu choked on his wine, laughing. Abrithil banged him roughly on the back. "All right, I'm fine," he said after many painful slaps from Abrithil's hand.

"You better be because if you're not, I'll have to slap you on the back several more times again." With that, they all laughed.

"So, Elizabeth," said Ryuu, "what's it like to live in royalty?"

With that, Elizabeth told him how she grew up as a princess. Melanie and Cassea also joined in on the conversation. They told each other stories of funny things that they did or what happened to them. They laughed, and they cried. Ryuu was even dumb enough to take a sip from his goblet just before the punch line of a joke that Melanie told and almost sprayed the three of them with wine.

Suddenly Abrithil quickly stood up, knocking his chair over. Ryuu, Elizabeth, Melanie, Cassea, and Queen Elaine jumped in their seats, completely bewildered.

"Excuse me," he said, and he left the table. Ryuu watched him as he went. Abrithil walked down to the far end of the hall where a man was waiting for him.

Ryuu jumped out of his seat. "I think I know that man," he said, "Yes, I do know him. He delivered my invitation."

"Uncle Christopher?" asked Elizabeth curiously. "Are you sure?"

"Yes, he ... Wait, did you say uncle?" said Ryuu, turning his attention to her.

"Oh, he's not our real uncle. We just call him that. He's an old family friend, you see. Oh dear, what are they arguing about?" Ryuu looked back at the king to see him stomp a foot in frustration, then he followed Christopher out of the hall.

BEING WITH YOU

It was some time before the king and the man returned to the festivities. Ryuu noticed a grim expression on Abrithil's face and wondered what was troubling him. But when he asked the king what was the matter, Abrithil just shook his head and said nothing. For a while, their table became uncomfortably silent. Abrithil seemed to attack his food with anger while the rest of them stared at him.

"Father?" asked Elizabeth warily. "Is everything all right?"

"What? Oh, yes. I'm fine," said Abrithil, blushing. "Sorry about all that."

Soon they were all in a cheery mood again and were talking about the upcoming fun and games that were going to be held for the next few days. They discussed archery contests, jousting tournaments, fencing duels, a javelin-throwing contest, and many other things. Ryuu was most interested in the jousting tournament, and they all had a long-winded discussion about it. There was also to be a magician demonstrating all sorts of wonderful magic tricks.

Soon after their discussion, gifts were brought out to the king and Ryuu. The king was given many gifts of gold, large gemstones—many were large sapphires—beautifully carved stone statues of the greatest detail, and a sapphire sword and dagger forged by Christopher himself. Ryuu received fewer gifts, but it was more than what he usually got at Voggna's place. He received a golden necklace that had a dragon head pendent from Elizabeth, a silver ring with sapphires that circled it from Melanie, an eagle feather to tie around his sword handle from Cassea, a bag of gold from Abrithil and Elaine, and a golden dagger with a black handle from Christopher, which was also forged by him.

"This blade will be forever sharp. Use it carefully," said Christopher.

"Thank you. I will," said Ryuu, admiring the golden blade.

Abrithil rose from his chair and announced, "My dear people of Riverside, thank you for coming on this glorious night of feasting." The crowd cheered in agreement. The king waved them down. "Yes, thank you again for coming tonight. I hope you all enjoyed this finest of meals." More cheers. "Now then, good night to all of you. The games begin early tomorrow afternoon at Lakeside, so wake up early to get there in time."

The crowd cheered again with excitement; little by little, the guests left the hall.

"We'll be leaving tonight, Ryuu, so if there's anything you need to do, do it now while you still have some time."

To Ryuu's surprise, it was Elizabeth who said those words. When he looked at her, she blushed. Abrithil chuckled and beckoned him to follow him. Ryuu did so and followed him out of the hall.

"It appears someone is already fond of you, Ryuu." Ryuu felt his ears go hot, knowing that they had just turned red. That made the king chuckle again. "Don't be embarrassed. She's been quiet lately. In fact, I think this was the first time I heard her speak in a long while. Maybe it's because she's been preparing herself to make a good impression to you."

"Why would she want to do that?" asked Ryuu, confused.

"Why?" The king chuckled. "Because you're the first prince to set foot in this castle, and she didn't know how to appear to you."

Ryuu felt puzzled. He had never dealt with this kind of situation before and had no idea how to approach her without embarrassing himself.

"You know, Ryuu, I can help you with this," offered Abrithil. "She is my oldest, and I think she would like to spend more time with you. *Alone*," he added seriously.

"Thank you," said Ryuu nervously.

"Don't worry. I'll give you some tips on the way to Lakeside."

It took over a half an hour to pack the wagon with the needed provisions for the overnight journey to Lakeside, which took them the rest of the night to get there. Many games were already set up and ready. Ryuu felt like watching the sunrise on a nearby hilltop before things began. In the distance, he saw a gigantic figure that rose above the early morning clouds.

"Beautiful, isn't it?" said Abrithil, joining Ryuu on the hilltop.

"What is that?" he asked the king.

"That," said Abrithil, "is Cyndrio Tower."

Ryuu looked at it in wonder. He knew of its existence but never knew how enormous it was. "How high is it?" he asked in amazement.

"I don't know," answered the king, "but that's the top of the tower." He pointed to the point where the tower touched the clouds and then added, "And its perimeter is about two-hundred and fifty miles around. I don't know much about the tower, but Christopher knows more than others do. He's said that he's actually been in the tower before and that he's been to the top of it too. I don't believe him though. Many questions about that place are still not answered. If you want to know more, just ask Christopher."

Ryuu shook his head in disbelief. "It sounds like a mystery not fully solved," commented Ryuu.

"That it is, Ryuu. That it is," agreed Abrithil.

The sun shone brightly in the blue morning sky. Servants were rushing back and forth, double checking to see if everything was ready and in place. Amid the turmoil, Melanie was practicing her archery for the opening shot to the archery contest. As Ryuu watched her from his chair from the royal stands, he witnessed her making three perfect bull's eyes.

"She's really good, your sister," he commented to Elizabeth.

She nodded. "She likes to shoot arrows in her spare time. That is a great elven bow that Uncle Christopher had the elves make for her eleventh birthday."

After Melanie made her fourth shot, Ryuu noticed that she scratched her right wrist. *It probably means nothing,* he thought to himself. But just then, Elizabeth scratched her own wrist in the exact same spot. But Ryuu ignored the gesture.

By early afternoon, the people of Riverside arrived. Soon all the stands were filled, and the games began. "Ladies and gentlemen," announced the herald, "the archery contest is about to begin!" The crowd cheered their enthusiasm. "Princess Melanie, will make the opening shot!"

Taking aim as she practiced earlier, Melanie made her shot and hit the dead center of the bull's-eye. The crowd cheered again as she left the field to sit next to her little sister, Cassea. The contest lasted for an hour and a half, for that game had the most combatants. When the game was over, Efgree Thomas was declared the victor, shook hands with the king, and was given the victory prize of three hundred pieces of gold. Efgree took the prize with delight and took off to find his wife in the crowd.

The fencing duels took up the rest of the day. Ryuu found it pretty boring and felt like leaving in the middle of it, but he thought it would be rude if he did. So he just sat there and pretended to enjoy the contest. Elkin Porik was announced champion and accepted his prize of three hundred pieces of gold with glee. Ryuu went back to the hilltop he stood upon before to watch the sunset.

"Did you enjoy the day?" asked a voice from behind. Ryuu turned to find Elizabeth standing there.

"Yes, I did," he said, not entirely truthfully. "You care to join me?" he asked, offering her his hand. Elizabeth blushed and with obvious delight, took his hand. "You look beautiful tonight," he said, feeling a bit dumb.

Elizabeth's cheeks seemed to turn even redder than before. "Is it true?" she asked. "Are you really from the fallen kingdom?"

Ryuu nodded. "I may be from the fallen kingdom, but I have never lived there," he said, "But someday I will return to my home, and I will return it to its former glory. I will remove the darkness that has plagued its streets. I will restore the light that has been shrouded by the darkness, and I will restore its throne."

"You really mean it, don't you?" asked Elizabeth, somewhat frightened.

"Yes, I do," answered Ryuu, "but I can't do it alone. There are others that I need to find to help aid me in my quest."

Elizabeth nestled herself beside him. "It's getting late. Look. The sun is almost below the horizon." Ryuu looked across the horizon, watching the sun disappear behind the trees. "Good night, Ryuu," whispered Elizabeth, hugging him.

"Good night, Elizabeth," he whispered back and then left the hilltop to his tent.

The next morning Ryuu woke with excitement, for the jousting tournament was to be held today. Stepping outside his tent, he went to watch the sunrise. He found Elizabeth waiting for him on the hilltop. "Good morning!" he called.

"Good morning," she replied, giving him a wide smile. "The sun is beautiful this morning," she said, looking at the horizon.

"It is," agreed Ryuu. Then blushing, he added, "As are you."

Elizabeth blushed. "Ryuu?" she asked in a soft voice.

"Yeah?"

"What is your home like?"

"Which one? Garindel or my master's temple?"

Elizabeth giggled. "The temple," she answered.

"Well," said Ryuu, "it's a beautiful place to live in. It has many gardens, mostly filled with flowers. There is a stable, a water fountain in the middle, fairies come occasionally, and the rest, well, it's mostly filled with books and empty rooms these days."

Elizabeth giggled again, and then sat beside him. "Tell me about the fairies." she said.

"All right," said Ryuu. "I'll tell you. At night, they glow many different colors of reds, blues, oranges, yellows, greens, and shades of purple. They flutter around the flower gardens and sing to them. Their melodies fill your ears and make you want to dance among them. Would you like to hear one of their songs?"

She smiled. "Yes, I would."

Ryuu nodded; then he began to sing. "Oh, come to me, oh curious ones. Lift up your heads to the morning sun. Let there be food and drink in the halls of Ambrintrink. Oh come and jump in the springs of Comrinnrink, for we love to splash in waters deep. Oh, join us now in glowing trees, we fairy kings of three, for we are brave and we are free. Oh come to me, oh curious ones. Come and see beyond the sun. Oh holy land with silver streams and mountains deep with billowing steam and fiery planes where phoenixes live in places far and skies where dragons are!" Thus he ended with a long note.

"You sing like an elf!" exclaimed Elizabeth, amazed by his voice.

"Thank you," said Ryuu, blushing.

"Do you sing often?" Elizabeth asked.

"No, I don't," answered Ryuu. "But I wish you could have heard the rest; it takes half a day to sing it in full."

"It's still beautiful," she said. "I've never heard anything like it."

Ryuu nodded. "Yes, it is beautiful." Looking at the sun, he added, "Come now. The others will wake soon, and the tournament will begin without us."

Elizabeth nodded and followed him back to the camp.

The tournament soon began, and the excitement was overwhelming. The knights of Riverside challenged each other in an epic battle of bravery. The competition went swiftly; the first match took less than a minute to finish. The final match would be against Sir Weiss, the previous year's champion. Ryuu asked many questions about the knights of Riverside, and Elizabeth answered him politely in turn. "Some say Weiss was the descendent of a high mage of Trilindo, the magic city. Some also say that he's the descendent of a Dragon Knight, but if he was, my father would know. He won't recruit anyone unless he knows their past experiences and heritage."

It seemed to Ryuu from what Elizabeth had told him that each knight came from Riverside or from foreign parts of Cyndroania. Sir Weiss was one of those knights from distant parts. In fact, he came from the other side of Cyndroania from the northeastern city Amrythilian. From what Ryuu knew, Amrythilian was a city built by warriors from all over Cyndroania. The construction of the city symbolized peace and unity among the many different races of Cyndroania.

The next match soon began with Sir Kole and Sir Ving. Then Sir Tinn and Sir Tan Li, and after them were Sir Min and Sir Ching. Ryuu thought there was something odd about their names, but he couldn't tell why. He was still trying to figure out what was so funny about the names by the end of the eighteenth match. By that time, it was time for lunch, and Ryuu soon forgot about his little puzzle. Once again, Ryuu and the royal family sat together at a reserved table. While they ate, magic users juggled balls of fire, made each other disappear and reappear again, made balls of light dance around their heads, and sword fought each other using their magic to control the swords. Minstrels played their music; performers acted out ridiculously funny skits that made absolutely no sense whatsoever. Storytellers told tales of old, and the people shared gossip with one another. An hour and a half later, the jousting tournament continued with its last five matches for the day, Sir Weiss being the winner again. When Sir Weiss received his winnings, everyone gathered their things to return to Riverside. On the way there, Christopher rode up to King Abrithil and beckoned for Ryuu to come closer so he could hear.

"I've taken the dragon eggs to the elves in Synaigwa to keep them safe from the enemy. They'll be safer there than at Voggna's temple, I assure you."

Ryuu looked at him confused. "Why would you need to do that?" he asked.

"Because," said Christopher, "from what my sources told me, the enemy is gaining back his power, and they believe that his first target will be Voggna's temple to steal the dragon eggs."

"What are you thinking of, Christopher?" asked Abrithil. "I know that look when I see it. Don't do anything rash now. Remember how upset Cybele was the last time you did something stupid?"

Christopher shot him an angry look. "I remember, Abrithil. You don't have to remind me about it. I'm going to head home tonight. I'll need some things for the journey back, and I was wondering if you could help me get some of those things for me."

Abrithil chuckled. "Of course, Christopher. Anything you'll need will be up at the castle."

Christopher nodded. "Thank you, my friend. Tell Storm that Cybele says hello and that she's doing well."

Abrithil chuckled again. "I will. Now get going."

Christopher sped off, leaving Ryuu with the king. "How does he know so much, Abrithil?" he asked. "I'm worried about Voggna."

Abrithil just shrugged and said, "I don't know, Ryuu, but he does tend to know more than he lets on. Why don't you ride next to Elizabeth and talk with her to let this pass from your mind."

Ryuu nodded and went over to Elizabeth and talked with her the rest of the way to Riverside, but something kept nagging at his thoughts. *How did Christopher know so much?*

A DANCE, A KISS, AND A VISION

As they trotted up through the forest path, Ryuu saw many packs of wolves that crept along in the shadows next to the company of people. He pointed this out to Elizabeth, and then she told her father, who said, "They're curious about what's going on, I guess. Don't worry. They won't attack us unless they feel threatened."

At that moment, the same silver wolf came up behind Ryuu and startled Elizabeth and the rest of the crowd. Abrithil cursed under his breath and bellowed at the wolf, "What did I tell you before, Silver Tail! You should know better! If you don't hurry, you'll miss Christopher at the castle! Well? Get a move on. Now!" The wolf gave him a glaring look with a growl and then sped on toward the castle.

"What was that all about, Father?" asked Elizabeth.

"Nothing, darling," said Abrithil, waving her away.

As they rode on, Ryuu spent as much time with Elizabeth as possible. His feelings for her were stronger than he thought. He just couldn't take his eyes off her. He noticed that Elizabeth kept blushing every time her father caught her looking at Ryuu, who kept chuckling in turn.

"Um, Lord Abrithil?" asked Ryuu to the king.

"Yes? What is it, my boy?"

"I was just wondering what we will be doing when we get back to the castle?"

Abrithil chuckled. "Do you not remember?" Ryuu shook his head. "Well, tonight we rest. Tomorrow we have the kingdom's ball." He chuckled again and turned to look at Elizabeth. "It may be dark out, but I can tell that you are blushing, Elizabeth."

Ryuu turned to look at her. Abrithil was right. Even in the dim moonlight, he could see that her cheeks were turning a rosy color. He smiled at her; she smiled back and then looked away, trying to hide her face from him. He turned back around in his saddle.

Within a few hours, Riverside castle came into view. They trotted along the path to the east gate, and once they were within the castle walls, the townspeople went their separate ways and returned to their homes. Ryuu and the royal family returned to the castle. Once inside, they left their horses in the stable and lingered to their rooms. Cassea was so tired; Ryuu actually carried her to her room. He held her gently as a loving brother would, tucked her in, and left her room, quietly closing the door. He said good night to Elizabeth, who hugged him in return, and Melanie scowled and stormed to her room. Ryuu cocked an eyebrow at this but didn't pursue the matter. Abrithil led Ryuu to the guest room on the bottom floor of the castle and told him that he would have the servants prepare a better room for him tomorrow and left the room. Ryuu stretched his arms, yawned, and threw himself onto the soft bed. A servant came in and left him some clothes to wear for the night. Sighing, he undressed himself, put the night clothes on, and fell asleep.

The next morning, Ryuu woke to a knocking at his door. "All right, all right, I'm up! Come in."

He got up and stretched as the servant from the night before came in the room and said, "Sorry if I woke you up, sir, but there is a feast that will taking place soon, and then the ball will be held a few hours afterward. The king would like you to have these since you're staying here for a while." The man placed two sets of tunics on a table next to the door. The servant bowed and left the room. Ryuu sighed and got out of bed. He went over to take a look at the tunics. One was royal blue with gold trim, and the other was black velvet with red trim. Each had matching pants and a white shirt that was worn underneath the tunic. Both were exceptional, and Ryuu had a hard time deciding which one to choose. He finally chose the black garment to wear to the ball and the blue one to wear to the feast.

The feast began at midday. All gathered in the great hall with great excitement. The tables had white linen cloths on them with fresh spring flowers as a centerpiece. These flowers turned out to be Ryuu's favorites, dragon hearts. The feast was as wonderful as the last feast Ryuu attended.

When the feasting was over, Ryuu went to his room to change for the ball. He put on the black velvet tunic. He looked at himself in the mirror and examined his features. He liked what he saw. His black hair was long, and his beard needed to be shaved. But he had to admit that he looked quite handsome. He wanted to look his best for Elizabeth. He smiled and left the room.

When he returned to the great hall, the tables were removed, an area was cleared for the minstrels, and there was ample room for dancing. Ryuu saw King Abrithil and Queen Elaine with their daughters and went up to them.

"You're looking good tonight, Ryuu! That tunic looks great on you!" said Abrithil.

"Thank you, kind sir," said Ryuu.

When Ryuu turned around, he saw the princesses still standing there, looking at him with dreamy eyes. *I wish I had younger brothers,* he thought to himself. *Still, Ryuu, don't make a fool of yourself. Stay calm.* Trembling, he approached the three girls. As he did, his scar started to tingle. The tingling got stronger with each step. Building up his courage, he said to them, "You all look very beautiful tonight."

Melanie and Cassea giggled but stopped when Elizabeth glared at them. "He's being serious, you two," she said sharply, but couldn't help smiling herself. "He gave us a compliment."

Melanie and Cassea looked down, pretending to look ashamed. "Thank you Ryuu. So do you, but handsome, not beautiful. It would sound strange to say that to a man, now wouldn't it?" she went on, blushing.

"Thank you, Elizabeth. Would you..." Ryuu stuttered for a moment and then continued, "would you like to dance with me?"

She curtsied and said, "Yes, I will. It would be an honor." She gave him her hand and said, "Come. I know the perfect spot."

Melanie watched them as they left. Ryuu thought he saw a glint of jealousy in her eyes. Ryuu's hand was starting to burn, and he tried his best not to react to it. Nevertheless, it hurt. Elizabeth had led him to the balcony. It was a wonderful place; he was able to see the land of Riverside from that very peek. Looking up, he could see the moon glint in the night. Somehow the place felt strangely romantic. Elizabeth headed over to the railing and said, "Isn't it wonderful up here, Ryuu? Every time I come up here, it feels so romantic. My mother and father were married on this very balcony, and I wish to do the same some day." Ryuu just looked at her and smiled. She blushed.

Ryuu walked over to her, joining with her at the railing. "Can you keep a secret for me?" he asked.

"Sure," she replied. "What is it?"

Ryuu wondered if he could trust her. Then he removed the gauntlet from his right arm and rolled up his sleeve to show her the scar on his wrist. Her eyes widened at the sight of it. "I was born with this. Every day I have to live with it. But I'm proud of it. It is my future and my past."

He pulled his sleeve back down, put the gauntlet back on, and looked back at Elizabeth.

"Easy for you to say," she said, trembling. "I have to live with a scar and not even know what it is!"

Ryuu jumped up right. "You have a scar too?" he asked, amazed.

"Yes, I do," she answered.

"Then let me see it!" She considered it for a moment and then showed him. Amazed, Ryuu had found the first of the eight chosen ones. The scar had a dragon's head with a tree on its forehead. "Do you know what it means?" Elizabeth asked.

"Yes!" said Ryuu, looking back up at her with excitement. "You're a chosen one! Does anyone else have a scar on their right wrist? Your sisters, do they have a scar?"

She thought of it for a moment and then said, "Not that I know of. So that's what it means. I'm a chosen one, but of what?"

"I'll tell you more later, maybe after the party. I don't want this information to reach the wrong ears." He wasn't sure why, but he had a strange feeling that they were being watched by someone in the shadows.

The music stopped playing, and then an announcer spoke over the crowd of guests. "May I have your attention please? We are now going to play one of our king's favorite melodies. Now find your partner, and let the real dancing begin."

Ryuu looked back to Elizabeth and asked, "Shall we dance, beautiful?"

She blushed, curtsied, and said, "Yes, we shall."

Through the corner of his eye, he saw Melanie sit down next to her sister Cassea with her arms crossed, looking annoyed. Then the musicians started to play their instruments, and everyone started to dance.

Ryuu took Elizabeth's hand and then put his arms around her waist. She put her hands on his shoulders, and they started to dance. To Ryuu's surprise, he was doing extremely well. He felt like he was gliding across the floor, never missing a beat. The song was just perfect. Ryuu looked into Elizabeth's eyes. Now that he could see them up close, he noticed that they were the shade of light emeralds. Suddenly, something had awakened inside him. He tried to ignore it, but no matter what he did, he could not escape the strange emotions that were raging inside him.

For what felt like an eternity, Ryuu and Elizabeth danced. They looked at each other. Ryuu smiled. Elizabeth smiled back. Ryuu didn't know what to do. He'd never felt the way he felt tonight. The two of them stopped dancing and looked at each other's eyes.

He was about to say something, but before he could, Elizabeth cut him off and said quietly, "Don't talk. Now is not the...."

She got closer to Ryuu; a powerful sensation made everything go quiet. Everyone stopped dancing. The music stopped playing, and all eyes were upon them. Ryuu became nervous. Before Elizabeth finished her sentence, she kissed him on the lips. As she did, a vision came to Ryuu.

He saw a man in an unfamiliar forest, standing before a wooden coffin. White peonies petals fell around him as they were carried through the wind, giving everything a sweet smell. The older man lifted his head. He was saying something, but Ryuu could not hear his words. As the vision continued, Ryuu tried to determine who the man might be. Ryuu shuddered because he realized the man was him. The man was older and battle worn. A wide scar ran between his eyes and across the bridge of his nose. His hair was much longer than it was now, and he also had a thin beard. Then the older Ryuu threw himself on top of the coffin, crying in grief. As the vision continued, the body inside the coffin came into view; it was the very same woman that was now wrapped in his very arms. He fell to his knees, and he too wept. Then the vision was over.

After the vision had passed, the crowd was still silent. Someone started clapping. Then more people joined them, and a roar crashed over the two of them. All the people were cheering with the sound of congratulation. She was in love, and he was in love. But he knew now how it would end.

Elizabeth let him go and said quietly, "I love you, Ryuu."

It took him awhile to find his voice. Then he quietly replied, "I love you too, Elizabeth." Looking over her shoulder, he saw Melanie storming off. Elizabeth noticed what he was doing and looked over her shoulder and saw Melanie. Turning back to him, she said with a frown, "I wonder what could be bothering Melanie? She's been acting strangely tonight." Ryuu frowned, a nagging suspicion started to form in his mind. "I think I know what's bothering her," he said.

"What?"

"I think she's jealous."

"Oh no. Come on, let's go get her and bring her back to the party. I hate to see her upset like this."

Ryuu nodded, and they went after Melanie.

After a time, they found her in a room crying with her head on a bed. "Melanie," said Elizabeth quietly, "are you all right?"

She turned her head toward them and said sharply, "What are you doing here?"

Ryuu cocked an eyebrow. "Well, if you're going to be that way. We followed you for a reason." She was about to interrupt him, but he raised his hand to silence her. "Listen," said Ryuu walking over to the bed and sitting next to her, Elizabeth did the same. "I know what's bothering you."

When she did not answer him, he put a hand on her shoulder, and his scar started to burn. She flinched at the contact. Feeling a bit guilty, he looked up at Elizabeth who shook her head, guessing what was on his mind. Ryuu relaxed a little, knowing that Elizabeth had no objections to what he was doing. "Listen, you're too young for me. Some day you'll find someone your own age who is just as handsome as me." She giggled at that. Ryuu had to smile. "Come now," he said. "Tonight's supposed to be a fun night. Cheer up, and let's have fun. Come with us now, and let us all dance together."

Helping her up, he took her hand and guided her back to the party. When the three of them got back, the musicians were preparing to start another song. "Hurry now. To the balcony, quickly," said Elizabeth. "I have an idea Ryuu," she continued. "You and Melanie can dance together for one song, while I dance with Cassea. Then, when the song is over, we switch partners."

"Brilliant, Elizabeth! That's a great idea. Now no one gets left out." Hurrying over to the balcony, Ryuu and Melanie prepared to dance. It was awkward for him, for she was only chest high to him. *No matter.* He thought to himself while putting his hands on her waist. She put her hands on his shoulders, and then they began to dance. Like before, Ryuu felt like he was flying across the floor with each step.

"Do you know this song, Ryuu?" asked Melanie after a time.

Ryuu shook his head. "No, I don't. What is it called?"

Melanie looked up at him with a twinkle in her eyes. "It's one of my favorite melodies. It is called "Seven Dragons of Power". I was hoping they would sing the lyrics to it. It's very beautiful."

Ryuu smiled and said, "I can imagine."

After the song had finished, Ryuu danced with Cassea, with Elizabeth, Melanie again, and then Cassea once more. He was having the time of his life. Just being there at the party made him feel important to others for the first time.

The party ended hours later, just before sunrise. As soon as the last of the guests left, King Abrithil went over to Ryuu, looking very angry. Ryuu got up slowly, feeling guilty. The king stopped before him and said with a deep, demanding voice, "You put on quite a show, Ryuu!" He paused to let the words sink in, then smiled brightly. "You two have made me the happiest man in all the land!"

Ryuu was stunned. It was so unexpected that he gaped at him. "You're not mad at me?" he asked, bewildered.

The king shook his head and chuckled. "No, I am proud of you. Most of all Elizabeth."

Elizabeth had heard this exchange, and tears of happiness filled her eyes, and she hugged her father. "Oh Father, thank you!"

Abrithil patted her on the back. "There, there now."

Ryuu felt like crying as well, but he couldn't tell why. Was it because he knew her fate? Or was it that he felt responsible for her death to come? He could not decide. Letting go of her father, Elizabeth said that she was going to go to her room to rest.

"Ryuu," called the king, "come! Let me show you around the castle while we wait for Elizabeth to come back down. Shall we?"

*It was almost midday, and Ryuu realized he needed to go back to Master Voggna's temple. "My lord, I—," but he was cut off by the king.

"My boy, you may just call me Abrithil."

Ryuu continued. "Sorry. Abrithil, I must be going back. My master must be worried sick about me."

Abrithil laughed. "My boy, that's already taken care of. I sent a letter to him this morning. He knows everything. Besides, what harm can come to you here, hmm? I told your master that you would be staying for a while, so you might as well stay, and"—he winked at Ryuu—"spend more time with Elizabeth."

Ryuu just blinked and said, "I don't know what to say. Thank you." He thought for a while and asked, "Where is she anyway?"

The king laughed and said, "Now that's a good question. Frankly, I don't know where she is. My guess would be..."—he thought for a moment—"in the library or still in her room. I'll have a servant find her for you." They bowed to each other and then parted ways.

LITTLE RED DRAGON

As Ryuu went down the hall, he found a servant that took him to the library. The two of them went by many rooms. A terrifying roar came behind one of them, shaking the walls and ceiling, making dust fly everywhere. Ryuu asked what it was but only got a shrug from the servant, who said, "I don't know what's down there. Not even the other servants know. Everyone is forbidden to go down there, even the queen! Only the king is allowed down there. Ah, here we are. This is the library."

The servant stopped at an empty doorway that led into the library. "I'll stay here so when you want to leave, I can take you to your dormitory."

Ryuu walked in. As he did, he noticed an old man sitting at a table with a pile of books. The man picked up one of them and then opened it. He sniffed the pages and then pulled the book away from his nose, looking at it as if it had a strange odor. Then he examined the back of the book and rubbed his fingers along the spine and said to himself, "Must be at least five hundred years old." Ryuu thought the man was crazy. The book looked fairly new to him.

As Ryuu went on, he noticed Elizabeth sitting at a table with a book in her hands. Next to her on the table was a little maroon dragon curled up in a ball. As he got closer, he could see the dragon in more detail. Little dark-yellow spikes ran down its back. Its tail had a sharp blade like armor at the end of it, but it was just bone protruding from its tail. Its wings were folded up and had shiny black claws.

"Hello, Elizabeth," he said. She looked up from her book and smiled. Ryuu sat down next to her. "That's an interesting dragon you have there. What's his name?" Ryuu asked.

"His name is Rexon. Fascinating little thing he is. One time I burned my hand, and when he touched it, it completely healed!"

"Do you know what kind of dragon he is?" Ryuu asked.

"Well, I was going to ask you I couldn't find it in this book. The closest thing that looks like him is a Pyra Pomlura dragon, but not everything matches up. All Pyra Pomlura dragons have hind legs with wings that grow on their forearms. But Rexon has wings that protrude from the back of his shoulders. It makes no sense."

Just as she finished, Rexon stirred, slowly lifting his head. He looked at Elizabeth for a while and then looked at Ryuu with droopy eyes. Then he slowly got up and stretched like a cat, quietly yawning and showing his ivory teeth. Curious, Rexon crept toward him, limping. Ryuu's mouth dropped dumbstruck, for on the dragon's belly was a visible red scratch that came from his right thigh to middle of his chest. Each line was about a half inch wide, and Ryuu didn't even want to know how deep each one was. Where he was lying before was a pool of blood.

"Oh my, Rexon, what happened to you?" asked Elizabeth, horrified. Rexon just cocked his head, puzzled, and then looked at his belly. He touched one of the scratches with the tip of his nose and then the wound glowed for a few seconds and stopped. Ryuu was amazed by the dragon, for where the scratch once was, there was nothing but his completely healed belly. No evidence of the scratch remained.

"He's amazing!" exclaimed Ryuu. "His healing abilities I mean." Rexon looked at him again and closed his eyes. For a full minute, Rexon's eyes stayed shut and then jerked open. Ryuu almost fell backward in his chair. The movement was so abrupt; it made his heart skip a beat. When he looked at Rexon again, the dragon was directly in front of him. His whole body was surrounded by blinding silver flames; his eyes were glowing golden yellow. "What the—"

He was cut off as something burned his chest. Ryuu yelped in pain, clutching at his shirt. Ryuu then realized that it was his necklace that was burning him. He frantically pulled it out, trying not to burn his hands. When he finally got it out, Rexon touched the necklace with the tip of his nose; his scar burned for a few seconds, but the heat subsided. The last thing Ryuu remembered was seeing the silver flames that engulfed Rexon fade away before blacking out.

STRANGE REFLECTIONS

Ryuu lay motionless on a bed. He was lying on a soft, cozy bed, with the smell of sweet, sticky honey in the air. But as comfortable as the bed was, his head was throbbing, and his scar itched.

Have we finally gotten up now? said a rough, deep voice. *You've been out for a day or two, and—*

"A day or two! But—"

I'm only kidding, you idiot. You were only out for an hour, said the voice. *For the chosen one of twilight, you aren't very smart or wise but exceptionally dim witted.*

Ryuu opened his eyes to find himself face-to-face with Rexon. Ryuu then realized that they were the only two in the room. He stared into the dragon's golden eyes and asked, "Are you the one who is talking to me?"

Rexon stared back at him with a blank expression, then Rexon said, *You catch on quick, Ryuu.*

Ryuu jolted upright, realizing that he was hearing the words more telepathically rather than hearing them physically. He blinked in surprise, not really believing what he had heard.

What? said Rexon. *Did you think I was as mute as a spider?*

Ryuu was so stunned; it took him awhile to find his voice again. "No, I didn't. So what happened?"

Rexon closed his eyes and then said in a soft voice, *I never thought that this day would come. I've waited for over two hundred years for this event to occur once again. What I just did was something that only a Draggonian Dragon can do, activate a Draggonian necklace. I've granted you the ability to understand the dragon language. You can speak to any dragon in your tongue or through your mind when you're away from each other.*

Ryuu's mind buzzed with questions. "You're a Draggonian dragon? They exist? Where do they live? How—"

He was cut off when Rexon blew a jet of flames from his mouth. Then Rexon said, *You remind me of someone every Draggonian hates and every dragon wants to kill!*

"Who is that person?" he asked.

I'll not say. The information might be very... Rexon paused for effect, *unpleasant.* He sounded very annoyed.

"Ryuu, how are you?"

Ryuu looked at the doorway. Elizabeth was standing there, smiling. He grinned, happy to see her. For a few agonizing seconds, not one word was spoken; then she went over to the bed. She sat down on the edge of the bed, now looking concerned.

"Are you all right, Elizabeth?" he asked. "What's wrong?"

She didn't answer right away. Ryuu was about to ask another question when he saw a flicker of movement behind her. He leaned over to get a better view.

"What?" Elizabeth asked, turning around.

"Nothing," he replied. He really thought he saw a bushy, furry, silver tail leave the room.

"Are you well, Ryuu?" asked Elizabeth.

"Yes, I'm fine, but why'd you ask?"

"You're ghost white." She held up a hand mirror for him to see, and he didn't know what he was looking at. There was a face in the mirror, but it was not his. What he saw was the face of a dragon. The dragon was silver, black, and gold; spikes ran down the back of its neck, and its eyes were strangely familiar. Two bright sapphire eyes looked back at him like they were his. They *were* his. Its facial expressions were exactly like his. They *were* his. He blinked, and then it was gone.

"Terrible, isn't it?" said Elizabeth.

"What? Oh yes, it is. But I'm fine," he said, puzzled.

He started to get up when Rexon jumped on his chest and said to him in his mind, *Deep within your heart, you know who and what you truly are.* Then he leapt off him and onto the floor and out the door.

"What? Hey, come back here, Rexon!" Jumping out of the bed, startling Elizabeth, he ran after the little dragon, only to stop at the door of the room when Rexon was nowhere in sight. Scramming down the hallway, he cried,

"Rexon, what did you mean by that? Come back here. Rexon!"

Elizabeth gripped him by the arm and asked, "What's gotten into you, Ryuu?"

Ryuu dipped his head, feeling very strange and confused. After a moment's hesitation, he said, "Like I promised, I'll tell you about the Dragon Knights."

They sat at a table that was in the middle of the room for over an hour. He first started with the history of the Dragon Knights and how they began. Then he told her about the eleven most powerful Dragon Knights and that each had a special element. Then he told her about the eleven dragon eggs that were at his master's temple and the eight other chosen ones he had to find and that she was the first.

"So. Two millenniums ago!" Elizabeth seemed a bit shaken.

Ryuu looked outside. The sun had set, and the stars shown brightly in the sky. "You should get some sleep, Elizabeth. The day is old, and I am weary."

She nodded. She got up from her chair, and he showed her to the door. "Good night, Ryuu," she whispered.

"Good night, Elizabeth," he said and closed the door behind her.

Later that night, he went over to the basin to wash. The basin was already filled with water. When he looked over the edge of it, he saw the same strange reflection of the black, gold, and silver dragon. He turned his head this way and that, but no matter what he did, the dragon's movements reflected his. Eager to get rid of the reflection, he threw his fist through the water. When the water dissipated, his reflection was normal again.

After Ryuu had washed, he went over and sat down by the fireplace. He was surprised that it was still burning considerably well after all the time he had spent in his room. The flames were still very high. While he sat, his thoughts kept returning to what Rexon had said.

"Deep within your heart, you know who and what you truly are," he muttered to himself. "Ah, but what did he mean by it?" He paused in his thoughts and then told himself, "Well, in any case, it doesn't matter. Tomorrow I'll leave for home and return to my studies." Rising to his feet, he walked over to the bed, tucked himself in, closed his eyes, and fell asleep.

TRAGEDY

Ryuu woke with a start. It must have been only a few hours before sunrise, yet there was something terribly wrong. Quickly rolling out of bed, he clothed himself in the garments he wore the night he first came to the castle, put the leather belt with the sapphire buckle on around his waist, strapped on his silver sheath and his amethyst sword, and then ran to the balcony. In the far distance, he could see a raging fire. The smoke was already looming high in the dimly lit sky. A wave of pure horror gripped him for he knew where the fire had started.

"Master, no!"

Running toward the door, he grabbed his traveling cloak and ran out of his room and down the spiral staircase two steps at a time.

When he reached the main floor of the castle, Rexon flew past him and said, *Follow me. Don't ask any questions. Just follow. There isn't time!*

Ryuu did what he was told. Rexon guided him through many corridors, turning down this hallway and that, never seeming to get tired from the frantic beating of his wings. Finally, they reached a wooden door; the smell of horses came from the other side. Ramming the door open, Ryuu ran from pen to pen, searching for Winter.

Rexon landed on a post of one of the pens and called, *Ryuu, over here!*

He ran over to him. When he saw Winter, he franticly fiddled with the latch to the pen; he was surprised but happy that he didn't have to saddle her. It was as if someone had done it for him. Jumping on her back, he guided her out of the stable. Once they were on the city street, Ryuu kicked his heels and bellowed, "Yah!" Winter whinnied and reared and then bounded through the city towards the gate. When he reached the city gate, the guards were already opening it, and he charged right through the gate. He imagined himself to be nothing but a blur as he passed them and onto the forest path.

Fear raced through Ryuu. *What could have started the fire? How could this happen?* The path that led to Spirit Field from Evergreen Forest passed them without notice. In fact, many things passed the two of them without a second glance. Now they were halfway across Spirit Field, almost to the entrance of Draggonian Forest. A few minutes later, the sight of the fire came into view. In the center of the blazing flames stood a man in black and purple armor. His black sword pointed down at a man on the ground. Ryuu climbed off Winter and quietly crept forward. He hid behind a pile of rubble and listened.

"Where are you hiding them, old man?"

Ryuu shivered. The voice sounded as if it was not human.

"I'll never tell you where they are! Never!" retorted Voggna. "I'd rather die than tell you their location."

Ryuu looked over the pile of rubble with pure horror.

"Then you shall be no more!" the man yelled in fury. Then he stabbed Voggna through the heart.

Ryuu could not contain himself any longer. He leapt from his hiding place, sword drawn, and charged at the man and bellowed, "Curse you!" Before he even came close to the man, he was swept off his feet by an unseen force. He was pushed back and slammed against a crumbling pillar, which almost broke on the impact. Ryuu fell to his knees, panting. He had never dealt with someone who could use magic. It took all his strength to stand back up again.

"Foolish of you, my young Dragon Knight. You should not face someone who's more powerful than you." The man pointed his black sword at him. Now that the man was closer, Ryuu recognized the sword. It was the same sword that was on Voggna's wall in his study. It was Blood Fang. The man stepped toward him, the sword now at his side, covered in the blood of Ryuu's master. "Now, perhaps you can help me?" asked the man.

Before the stranger got within three feet of him, something buzzed past Ryuu's left ear. In that split second, an emerald-colored arrow imbedded itself in the stranger's right shoulder, right between the joints. He staggered for a moment, clutching at his shoulder and howled in agony. Then another buzz passed Ryuu's ear, and the stranger blocked the arrow with his sword. Then the stranger jumped, flipping backward in the air. Then another man, Ryuu guessed about a few years older than him, jumped past him. In his hands was a foot and a half wide, four foot long sword. The edges of the sword were dark emerald green; the rest of the sword was bright silver. The man wore black and green armor. A dark green cape flowed down his back, supported by a silver chain. Long black hair ran down a little past his shoulders. A scar streamed across his left cheek. The stranger got to his feet. His hood fell, revealing his face. Ryuu looked away, terrified. The stranger's face was pale white; a terrifying scar ran across his right eye. His hair was short and spiky and black as ashes. His eyes were bright crimson.

The man next to Ryuu said loudly, "Leave this place, Mávro Dráko, for you are wasting your time!" Ryuu looked up at the man before him. He knew that voice. "Christopher?" Without taking his eyes off the man named Mávro Dráko, he gave Ryuu a slight nod, then continued warning Mávro Dráko. "What you are looking for is no longer here. The dragon eggs are in a safer place! Leave now, or be destroyed!"

"You," said Mávro Dráko. "Curse you! May you one day be slain by my blade! May you die a horrible, merciless death! I have dealt with you long enough!"

"Your father has already prevented that from ever happening!"

Christopher readied himself to fight. Ryuu got to his feet and went to him. Then suddenly, Christopher swung his sword in front of him, blocking his way. Ryuu looked at him, and Christopher looked back at him over his shoulder. Ryuu understood. *He wants me to leave.* Ryuu nodded and then darted toward Winter, jumped on her back, and galloped away through the night.

As Ryuu charged through the forest, he never looked back. He was afraid. It was the first time he was truly afraid of what was going to happen. He didn't know where to go. The only home to him now was at the Riverside castle. He rode on and was halfway across Spirit Field when Christopher came galloping up beside him and said, "Keep going. We need to get to the castle."

Daybreak soon arrived, bringing life to the world, but it didn't ease the aching pain in Ryuu's chest that was his heart. When they arrived at the castle gates, no guards stopped them from entering. They brought their horses to the stables, ignoring the pages who offered to take care of the horses for them. When Christopher got off his Friesian, he pulled something off its back. It was the size of a man, all wrapped up. Ryuu knew who it was and dipped his head. Tears filled his eyes, and he leaned against a stable post. Christopher carried Voggna's body out of the stable and into the castle. Ryuu followed.

The two of them walked silently through the castle. As they went, some people followed, some gasped, and some stared. Ryuu was melancholy; he didn't even notice Rexon land on his shoulders.

"Ryuu, what's going on?" someone asked him.

Ryuu thought that it was Elizabeth and looked up. It was. He tried to speak to her, but the words wouldn't come out, and he lowered his head. They finally reached a circular room with a stone table in the center. On the table were many pieces of wood. Christopher placed Voggna's body on the stone table, knelt on his knees, and bowed his head. The group of people waited outside of the room.

When Christopher got back up again, he walked to the door, closed it, and slid the bolt on the door to the locked position. Then he grasped a torch off the wall and lit the stone table. Then the cremation of Ryuu's master began. And so it was of Master Voggna, the Dragon Master.

COUNCIL OF THE SPIRITS OF OLD

Many hours passed during the cremation. Ryuu watched as the man he once loved and respected burned before his eyes. The same man who raised him, the same man who cared for him, and the same man who was like a father to him during his youth. Ryuu was so distraught that nothing else existed but him and the burning man before him. When the flames died out, only a pile of ashes remained. Christopher stood up and spoke in an unfamiliar language. When he finished, a brilliant gold gem replaced the black ashes on the stone table. The gold gemstone was as big as his hand. Its light was so beautiful that the gem seemed to be alive. Christopher picked up the gemstone from the table and handed it to Ryuu.

"Take it," he said. "It is yours. I'll tell you what to do with it later."

Ryuu looked at the gemstone for a minute and then put it in his pouch. Then Christopher went back to the stone table and muttered in the same strange language from before. Then the stone table slowly lowered into the floor. Once it was completely in the floor, Christopher said to Ryuu, "Come."

Ryuu obeyed. As soon as Ryuu's foot touched the top of the stone table in the floor, the light from above them vanished, leaving the room in darkness. Then a ring of light surrounded the two of them. A voice from the darkness called out to them, "Oh mortal of Cyndroania, why have you summoned us? Name thy self."

Christopher spoke. "It is I, Guardian Dragon Knight Christopher, son of none, surviving member of the old order, Dragon Knight of nature." When he finished, nine rings of light surrounded the two of them. Then nine figures appeared out of thin air. They each wore black and gold robes. They each removed their hoods to reveal ghostly figures of three different races. The first three were of a dragon-like race. The second group of three was of humans and the last group of elves. Ryuu looked at the dragon-like creature that was in the middle of its group.

The creature spoke. "I, King Garindel of the Draggonians, speak for my race."

Draggonians! Ryuu thought to himself with excitement. Then the man in the middle of the human group spoke, "I, Arrolonn, son of Virc, speak for my race."

Then the elf from the middle of their group spoke, "And I, Ultprye, son of Jexc, speak for my race."

After the representatives announced themselves, King Garindel spoke. "As the leader of the high council, I give you, Guardian Dragon Knight Christopher, son of none, permission to ask us for our guidance. But first, tell us what has befallen you these past few months."

Christopher bowed and told him of the recent occurrences. Ryuu had no idea what he was saying, for he spoke in the same strange language. Then Christopher said, "Last night, Voggna's temple was attacked and destroyed by the new Shadow Knight, Mávro Dráko." The council members gasped and muttered to one another in their groups. "I am not finished," announced Christopher. "I have more to tell." Silence engulfed the room. "Master Voggna is dead, and my nephew Ryuu was unable to complete his training, and I don't know how to deal with the situation at hand. Please, almighty high council, will you help me?"

Ryuu was shocked. *I'm not alone!* "You're my uncle? But how… I mean, I never knew. I never suspected."

Christopher grasped his shoulders and said, "Yes, I am your uncle. You are one of the only family I have left."

Ultprye stepped forward and said, "We have decided on what you must do, Christopher. Because of Voggna's death, you are responsible for the completion of Ryuu's training. You will teach him our secrets, our skills, and our history. You will teach him to speak in thy languages three: Draggonian, Elvish, and Sennohian. You are responsible for your nephew survival."

Christopher bowed and said, "I understand. Thank you for your time." The high council members bowed in return and vanished.

The room regained its normal appearance. Ryuu looked down and asked, "Why?"

"What?" asked Christopher.

"Why wasn't I told of you? Why did Voggna never tell me about you?"

Christopher shrugged and replied, "I don't know. I guess I guessed wrong. I thought you already knew about me."

Ryuu reached behind his back when he felt something shift on his neck. "Rexon, I forgot about you."

Rexon yawned and said, *Good morning, Ryuu. It's good to see you again, Christopher. I thought I wouldn't see you for another hundred years. When was the last time we met?*

Christopher laughed a hearty laugh and then said, "I believe it was about one hundred years ago."

"A hundred!" Ryuu could not contain himself. "How old are you exactly?"

Christopher thought for a while and then said, "Two hundred and fifty-three years old." He paused for a moment and then added, "Come to think of it, my birthday was just last month, so I'm actually two hundred and fifty-four years old."

Ryuu's jaw dropped in amazement. It was such a large number, he didn't believe him. Rexon laughed. Thinking about what had just occurred, Ryuu asked Christopher, "What were those, *things,* earlier?"

Christopher raised an eyebrow. "Could you not tell by their ghostly images what they were?"

Ryuu shook his head. "I didn't know what to make of it."

Christopher sighed. "They were spirits of old. Dragon Knights can call upon these spirits for help and guidance. You were lucky today, Ryuu."

Ryuu blinked. "How so?"

"You got to see the greatest Draggonian king of all the land. *Garindel.* He rarely answers to the summoning. He is one of the oldest of our order; in fact, he started the order along with his brothers."

An explosion broke the silence. They froze, not knowing what to do. "No. No it can't be!" yelled Christopher. He turned around and used magic to unlock the door which opened with bang as it hit the wall. Christopher grasped his sword from his back and ran through the opened door.

"Christopher!" yelled Ryuu. "What's wrong?"

Christopher stopped and looked over his right shoulder at him and said, "Draw your sword. He's here." Just as he finished, a gigantic boulder came through the wall and hit Christopher from the left side and through the opposite wall. When the dust cleared, he was nowhere to be found.

GOLD BLADE, BLACK BLADE

"Christopher! Christopher!" Ryuu cried out.

It's too late now. In the meantime, I'll look for the princesses, said Rexon.

"Then go, and hurry! Time is of the essence."

Rexon jumped off his shoulder and flew away. As he watched, a light shone behind him from the room he was just in. Ryuu turned around and saw King Garindel's spirit appear within, but it looked different from before, with two more sets of horns, which were all black now.

"Come," he said. "Come and take your inheritance and become what you were born to be." He drew a black and gold and silver sheath from his robes.

Ryuu ducked as an explosion came from behind him. He ran with all his might, nearly getting covered by debris. Then an explosion happened right in front of him. Ryuu lunged forward, barely making it into the room. He skidded across the floor, scraping his cheek. The room went pitch black as debris piled up in front of the door, trapping him inside. King Garindel stood motionless as he waited for Ryuu to take the sword. Ryuu got to his feet and walked over to him. When he stood in front of the king, he looked into his eyes and noticed that they were the same shade of sapphire as his. Garindel pointed the hilt of the sword at Ryuu, allowing him to draw it from its sheath. Ryuu hesitated for a moment and then drew the sword. As he did, a magnificent golden blade came from the sheath. Ryuu instantly recognized the sword. It was Destiny, the sword of light. The same sword his father used. Ryuu took the sheath from the king's hands and belted it onto his back. Then Garindel vanished, and Ryuu was left in darkness. Ryuu closed his eyes, and felt a wave of power emanating from the sword. He opened his eyes and reached into his pouch and pulled out the golden gemstone which was glowing bright yellow. On the sword's cross guard was a hole that matched the size of the gemstone in his hand. Ryuu placed the gem in between the hole, and as if the sword was alive, it clamped onto the gem, holding it in place. The blade shimmered with light. A vision flashed before him, and he saw a black, gold, and silver dragon with a knight on its back.

The dragon drew closer, and the knight held out his hand and said one word. "*Ready?*"

Ryuu grasped his hand, and the vision passed. The next thing he knew was that he was high in the air and was rapidly gaining altitude. Ryuu almost panicked; the sense of weightlessness overcame him. He looked up and saw the ceiling above him getting bigger and bigger by the second. He closed his eyes, preparing for a deadly and bloody impact; but it never came. He felt the wind blow past him. Ryuu opened an eye and was startled that he was standing on the roof of the tower. Curious of what had befallen Rexon, he held onto his Draggonian necklace as if he already knew what to do and thought, *Rexon.* He felt Rexon's thoughts brush against his mind and felt his curiosity of his call.

Yes? Rexon asked.

Excited that it had worked, Ryuu asked Rexon, *Rexon, have you found the princesses yet?*

Rexon replied, *Yes, but hurry. They need you. They're in great danger!*

I know! he said as he jumped off the roof top onto the next one far below. *I'm on my way!*

Ryuu leapt from this roof and that, never losing his footing. He couldn't comprehend what was happening to him. He felt so alive. His vision was enhanced, his hearing was improved, and he was faster than normal. Once he reached the street, people ran this way and that, screaming. Mothers held their children; their husbands held swords and shields. Baskets of food, tipped over wagons, and trampled outdoor markets littered the streets. Ryuu looked up to the castle. Smoke billowed out of giant holes in the side of the once-mighty walls of the castle. Ryuu's eyes bulged with outrage.

"Whoever you are, I'm going to kill you." He looked down at his feet and closed his eyes. Ryuu slowly gripped the hilt of his amethyst sword and slowly drew the blade. With both swords in hand, Ryuu darted forward toward the castle. As he did, he saw what the people were running from. It was a giant monster that could not have been from this world. It had the body of a dragon, but its head was more of that of demon. Ryuu was about to help fight the fiend, when a strong hand grabbed his shoulder and prevented him from going. Ryuu spun around to face a man with long, ginger hair and wearing a crimson tunic with black armor. "Let me and my friends handle this," said the stranger. "Go. This is beyond your strength. You won't survive a minute against that thing. The princesses are waiting." With a nod, Ryuu redirected himself toward the castle.

Rexon laid his head down on Cassea's lap, wishing that she could understand him.

"Elizabeth," said Cassea, "I'm scared. Where's Daddy?"

Elizabeth didn't answer. She stood motionless, holding her sword in front of her, looking toward the door. This was a special sword. It was given to her on her seventeenth birthday. The sword was made from the finest metal. Abrithil told her that it was specially made for her by the Draggonian's nova metal. The blade was the color of iridescent jade, while the hilt was made of the finest silver star, another type of Draggonian metal.

"Elizabeth?" Cassea whimpered.

"I don't know, Cassea," she replied.

"But...but I'm scared." Cassea looked as if she was about to burst into tears.

Without looking at her, Elizabeth said, "Don't worry. Everything is going to be all right."

Rexon raised his head from Cassea's lap and looked at the door with pure horror. Melanie noticed his reaction, drew an arrow from her quiver and knocked it to her bowstring, aiming it toward the door. An unearthly voice came from the other side of the door along with a loud boom. Elizabeth jumped out of the way in the nick of time, for the door flew past her. Melanie shot an arrow through the doorway. Not a moment later, she was thrown off her feet and slammed against the wall behind her, knocking her unconscious.

"Melan..." Elizabeth froze.

A man in black and purple armor walked into the room, holding a black sword in his right hand; a dragon of shadowy black and purple flames sat on his shoulder. The man raised his left hand, muttering words of power. Swinging his arm to the side, Rexon was thrown through the window. Cassea screamed in terror. The man spoke, his words deathly cold, like a snake hissing. "Do not cry. You're in no harm."

He stepped toward her and then stopped when Elizabeth cried, "Leave her alone!"

The man looked at her, sneered, and said, "My you are a pretty one. Perhaps you can help me." He stepped toward her now, holding out his hand. Elizabeth backed away. "Where's your father?" The man was now pointing his sword at her.

"I don't know!" she screamed. "I don't know! Leave me alone!"

The man threw his head back and laughed. Then out of the blue, a sword pressed against the man's chin.

"If it's me you want, then here I am," said Abrithil. Then without warning, the man swung around, hitting his blade against Abrithil's sapphire sword. As soon as the two blades met, the two of them vanished.

"Father!" both Elizabeth and Cassea screamed. Just then, another man burst into the room.

"Ryuu!" Elizabeth jumped up and hugged him. He would have done the same if he wasn't holding the two swords in his hands. "I was so worried. Where have you been? What's going on?" She let go of him.

"Now's not the time for stories," said Ryuu. "Right now we need to get out of here. Is there another way out? A secret door or something that can get us to the courtyard faster?"

Elizabeth nodded. "Yes, follow me."

"Wait!" exclaimed Ryuu, sheathing his amethyst sword. "What happened to Melanie?" Running over to her, Ryuu picked her up and slung her over his shoulder so he would be able to use his sword when needed. He nodded and then followed Elizabeth through the door. As he did, he stopped and turned around and said, "Come, Cassea. I'm here now. There's nothing to fear. I'll protect you."

Jumping off her chair, she ran to Elizabeth and held her hand.

Coming to a stop, Ryuu and the princesses stood before a stone wall. One of its bricks stood out more than the rest, but just by a little. Elizabeth pushed on it, and a secret path was revealed. A staircase ran down its length.

Cassea held Elizabeth's hand tighter. Then Ryuu took the lead, and they walked down the stairs, one by one.

As they walked, Ryuu asked, "How long has this been here?"

Elizabeth just shrugged and replied, "It must have been here ever since the construction of the castle."

"And it leads to the courtyard?"

"Yes."

"Then let's hurry!"

After what seemed like hours, Ryuu and the princesses finally made it to the courtyard where two dragons were fighting. Below the two dragons was the man in black and purple armor and King Abrithil. Ryuu could not believe his eyes. He recognized the dragon to the left—Lord Mávro Dráko's dragon, the same one from his visions.

The dragon beside Abrithil had scales black as the night sky. Its chest and belly were the same color of lightning blue. A sapphire sphere was engraved on its forehead; its eyes were as blue as the sea. Neither dragon attacked one another, but only circled their two masters, giving them enough room to fight.

"Be gone, you fowl traitor! Be gone and never return to my castle!" bellowed the king.

Lord Mávro Dráko laughed and said, "After I'm done here, there won't be a castle to return to!" Then he charged toward King Abrithil.

Ryuu noticed that the king was losing ground. His strikes got slower; his arms kept giving way. Abrithil wasn't going to make it. Then with a flash, Mávro Dráko dodged a vertical slash from Abrithil and drove Blood Fang through his chest. With a roar, Abrithil's dragon rushed toward him. Gripping his master with his front paws, he lifted him skywards and flew into the smoke above. Mávro Dráko cursed and ordered his dragon to follow and then turned to face Ryuu.

"So we meet again, my young Dragon Knight. Are you ready for round two?"

Leaning Melanie against a wall, Ryuu drew his amethyst sword.

Melanie slowly rose to her feet, groaning. "What happened?"

With his back to the princesses Ryuu said, "Go. Leave now while you still can."

Elizabeth stepped toward him. "But—"

"Go while there's still time."

The princesses left without another word. He walked toward Mávro Dráko and said, "I'm at a disadvantage. You can use magic, but I can't. To make things fair, you mustn't use magic against me. Am I clear?"

Mávro Dráko laughed. "Then you will use only one sword."

Ryuu nodded. "Agreed."

Sheathing his amethyst sword again, he held Destiny before him backhanded, with it blade pointing towards the ground, his wrist just above the cross guard. This was the first time he had used a sword since his master suffered a terrible heart attack during one of their duels. Now he would have to fight a true fight. A fight to the death. With Destiny's long hilt, he was able to hold the sword with both hands. Without warning, Ryuu lunged forward. The two swords collided with a deafening clash. Sparks flew. Both Ryuu and Mávro Dráko jumped back from each other; Mávro Dráko jumped back toward Ryuu, flipping in the air on his side with his sword outward. Landing on his feet, the two blades met once again. Ryuu staggered a bit from the impact and then spun around, striking Mávro Dráko's sword again, knocking him back. Running toward him, Ryuu jumped upward, planning to hit him from above. Mávro Dráko spun around and swung his sword upwards, stopping Ryuu in place. Pushing him back up, he swung around again, and the impact of his strike forced Ryuu to go flying into the sky. Ryuu looked down and saw that Mávro Dráko had jumped up to fight him in the air. Swinging his sword, he and Mávro Dráko struck each other's swords in a tireless frenzy. Each strike left sparks that fell beneath them as they ascended into the night sky. Then with one last strike, they moved closer to each other and locked their swords between their chests.

"Good form, Dragon Knight," mocked Mávro Dráko. "But no matter how hard you fight, you'll always fail in the end. Mark my words, Dragon Knight, you'll fall like the rest of your kind."

"No!" Ryuu pushed off and then slashed downward, tearing through Mávro Dráko's armor. Mávro Dráko howled in agony as the blade cut through his chest. With a kick, Mávro Dráko fell back toward the courtyard far below. As they fell, the ground seemed to rush up to them. Mávro Dráko landed on his back, clutching his chest. Ryuu landed heavily on his feet, crouched, and thrust out a hand to keep his balance. Standing up, Ryuu limped toward Mávro Dráko.

Without warning, Mávro Dráko abruptly rose to his feet, screaming, "Healoro!" With a flash, his wound healed, leaving nothing but a scar. Mávro Dráko looked at Ryuu with a sneer and then said, "Until we meet again, Dragon Knight."

Then black shadowy flames burst out of the ground, engulfing him in its darkness. The flames vanished, and Mávro Dráko was gone.

RESURGENCE

Ryuu stepped toward the spot where Mávro Dráko had been just seconds earlier. "Where are you?" he cried out, "Show yourself, you coward!" Nothing.

Ryuu looked up and noticed a dragon fly away in the night sky. As it did, a black feather fell from the sky. He held his hand out to catch it. The feather landed perfectly in his out stretched hand. Just then a loud explosion came from his right. An army of strange dragons came through an opening in the wall. Roaring in frustration, Ryuu charged them head on. Destiny seemed to glow even brighter than before. The creatures hissed in anger at the light. Ryuu jabbed Destiny toward them. As he did, they hissed and backed away. He grinned. Now that he knew their weakness, he ran toward the stable, keeping Destiny in front of him.

When he got there, he whistled for Winter. When she did not come, he went looking for her. When Ryuu finally found her, she lay in a pool of blood. "No. Winter."

Many scratches and bite marks covered her now mangled corpse. Ryuu fell to his knees. She was given to him on his eleventh birthday from Master Voggna. The loss struck him harder than he expected now that Voggna was dead. Ryuu stood back up to search for another horse. There were none. Just as he was about to leave, Christopher's Friesian trotted up to him. Without hesitation, Ryuu jumped onto his back. The Friesian began to gallop without a command.

Before long, Ryuu and Christopher's stallion caught up with the refugees from Riverside castle. Before Ryuu joined the crowd of people, Rexon landed on his shoulder and announced, *The king is safe. His wounds are healed, and he is getting better.*

Ryuu nodded. "Where is he now?"

Rexon lowered his head and said with remorse, *I can't tell you.*

"But why?" asked Ryuu. "What about the princesses and the queen? They need to know."

Rexon sighed and then said, *He asked me not to. I'm sorry, but I had no choice. He made me swear that I wouldn't tell anyone where he is.*

Ryuu lowered his head and said, "I ... I understand. So where to now?"

Rexon cocked his head in thought. *I think,* he said, *Oakwin will be the safest place to go. With a group this large, however, it might take a week and a half to get them there safely.*

"I can see that," said Ryuu. Then he asked, "What is Oakwin anyway?"

Rexon answered, *Oakwin is fortress where men go to train to become knights, practice with their swords, and sign up for the army. Oakwin has also survived many sieges.* Rexon sighed. *I could tell you everything about it, but once we get there, you will be able to see for yourself the glory of Oakwin.*

"I see. So we travel toward Oakwin," said Ryuu. "You will help me lead the way." It was not a question but a command.

Rexon nodded and flew off his shoulder. Heading to the front of the group of people, Ryuu found the princesses safe and sound. He sighed in relief and trotted toward them.

"All hail, princesses of Riverside! All hail, Queen Elaine!" he bellowed.

The crowd echoed his chant, "All hail, princesses of Riverside! All hail, Queen Elaine!"

Princess Elizabeth turned in her saddle to face him, a confident smile on her face; then she frowned.

"What's wrong?" he asked as he trotted along side her.

"Where's my father? Is he all right?"

"He's alright, but I don't know where he is. I'm sorry."

Shocked, Elizabeth asked, "Then how do you know that he's all right?"

"Rexon told me." She cocked an eyebrow but said no more.

After a few minutes had passed, Elizabeth asked, "Isn't that the horse Christopher was riding into the castle earlier in the day? Where's your white horse?"

"When I got to the stables, and I called out to Winter. When she didn't come, I went looking for her. When I found her, she was dead. Just as I was going to leave without a horse, Christopher's horse came up to me. So without hesitation, I jumped on his back and went looking for you and the others."

Landing on Ryuu's shoulder, Rexon said, *We should stop here for the night. We have many miles ahead of us tomorrow.*

Ryuu nodded. Heading toward Queen Elaine, he said, "My lady, we should stop here for the night. The people look tired and weary. We should make camp."

The queen thought it over for a bit and then said, "I agree, Ryuu. We should make camp. Now I have a favor to ask of you."

Ryuu frowned and said, "Anything you wish of me, my lady."

She nodded. "In the absence of my husband, will you take his place in his stead, Ryuu Dragonfang?"

"Me? But, why?"

"Because you are a prince, Ryuu, and we need a leader in his stead. Now I ask you again, will you take his place?"

"But why can't you m'lady?"

"Because," said the queen, "this is a chance for you to know how to be a leader and to take hold of your authority. Now please, Prince Ryuu, will you do it?"

Not knowing what to do, he lifted his chin and said with pride, "It will be my honor, my lady. I will take up the responsibility." Spurring the Friesian to the very front of the crowd, he stopped at the top of a hill so that all could see. "People of Riverside!" All eyes turned toward him, giving him their full attention. "We camp here tonight. We have traveled far enough today. Tomorrow we journey to Oakwin."

Someone in the crowd spoke. "Who the devil do you think you are ordering us about, you tyrant?"

Ryuu sighed. "If you must really know my name, then remember it well, for I shall say it only once. My name is Prince Ryuu Dragonfang, chosen one of twilight, the new leader of the old order, the Dragon Knights!"

The same person spoke again. "Hah! I'd rather believe our king is a Dragon Knight than you!"

Ryuu laughed. "For your information, he *is* a Dragon Knight!" He paused to see if anyone would object. After a minute had passed, he spoke. "Your queen has asked me to take your king's place in his absence. I expect you to give me the same respect as you would to your king and queen and their daughters. Now rest easy tonight. We have many miles ahead of us tomorrow morning."

Without a word, the people put their belongings aside and prepared to make camp.

JOURNEY TO OAKWIN

The next morning, Ryuu woke with a start. Sweat beaded his face. He had just had another one of his nightmares. Looking around his tent, he noticed that Rexon was sleeping next to him. Trembling, he went outside; it was nearly daybreak, and all was quiet.

"Guess I'm the only one who's up." He was cold, so he went over to the campfire to warm himself. Some freshly cooked meat sat next to the fire in a small bowl. Ryuu looked at it, puzzled. Crouching by the fire, he heard a rustling of grass nearby. Looking around, he saw that it was Elizabeth carrying a small bucket of water.

"Good morning!" he called.

Elizabeth jumped in surprise. "Oh, good morning, Ryuu. You startled me."

Ryuu cocked an eyebrow. "How long have you been up, Elizabeth?"

Sitting next to him, she put the bucket next to her and curled up, wrapping her arms around her legs and putting her chin on her knees, and then answered, "I've been up for a few hours now."

"Why? Is something bothering you?"

When she didn't answer, he crossed his legs and took a piece of meat from the bowl and took a few bites out of it. After a few minutes had passed, Rexon trotted to Ryuu's side and coiled up and laid his head on Ryuu's lap, his golden eyes looking up at him. Ryuu stroked his head affectionately. Rexon closed his eyes, smiling, and hummed.

A few hours later, people started to get up. Fires were set a blaze, and food was passed out. They ate and drank happily, but there was sorrow in their eyes. When the sun was set high in the sky, people started gathering their things. Once everybody had packed their belongings, the great host of people began their journey to Oakwin.

Ryuu could not remember how many leagues they went on their first day of traveling when they made camp that night, nor the next day or the day after that. All that he could remember was that he was tired—tired of their journey, tired of his new responsibilities, tired of not being able to sleep through the night, tired of the past few days.

"How much farther, Rexon?" he asked on the seventh morning of their pilgrimage.

We're making good distance each day. I believe at the rate we're going, we will be there in a day or two. Rexon grinned, exposing his ivory teeth and said to him in his mind, *You've done well, Ryuu.*

Ryuu got to his feet and walked outside his tent. Next to the tent was his new Friesian, Arrolonn. During one of the days traveling with him, he rummaged in Christopher's saddlebags. Inside one was a letter to him saying:

> Ryuu, this is Arrolonn. I give him to you, my nephew. He is the finest war horse you could find. Arrolonn wasn't my true steed, but he came in handy from time to time. He's yours now.
> Your uncle,
> Christopher.
> P.S.: You're not alone.

Ryuu didn't know what Christopher really meant by, "You're not alone," but he didn't dwell on it.

"Good morning, Arrolonn. Just a few days more, okay?" Arrolonn whinnied affectionately. "Yes, good boy. You've done well." Stroking Arrolonn's muzzle gently, he looked at the Draggonian Forest. He jumped. Standing in the shadows of the edge forest were two black and gold Draggonians. As he watched them, they watched him. Then without warning, they returned to the shadows of the forest.

Who were they? Ryuu asked Rexon.

They are Princes Polpenrir and Sylrir. It is the first time in eighteen years they have been seen. They've been looking for the chosen ones from the Dragon Knight Prophecy. They're on the same quest you're on. He paused and then said, *We must be off now. I'll tell you more about them later.*

That following afternoon, Oakwin finally came into view. The crowd roared with excitement as they beheld the mighty city. "We made it!" Ryuu exclaimed, "People of Riverside, we sleep in comfort tonight!"

The crowd roared even louder than before, cheering their triumph. "Well done, Prince Ryuu. Well done indeed!" said the queen. "Now let's get a move on so we can be in the city's walls by nightfall."

As they entered the mighty city, the hoard of people from Riverside was shepherded to many reserved inns for them. Somehow, they knew they were coming. Ryuu and the royal family were brought to the grand City Hall, where they were given private rooms of their own. Slouching on his bed, Ryuu moaned in relief.

You did well, Ryuu, said Rexon, tiredly.

I did, didn't I? said Ryuu, yawning. *You know, I'm leaving tomorrow, Rexon. I need to find those other chosen ones. Without them, the balance between light and dark will never rebalance itself. Oh, but where to look? I don't know where to start. I wish Christopher were here. He'd know what to do.*

Trust in your heart. Only then you will find the answers you seek. I will be there to guide you along the way Ryuu. Remember, you are not alone, said Rexon.

Dazed, Ryuu looked at Christopher's letter again. It was one of the last things that he had to remember him by. He read it five times before he turned it over. Surprised, there was another message on the back that echoed Rexon's word from earlier. *Deep within your heart, you know who and what you truly are.*

Hey, Rexon, what did you mean by deep within your heart, you know who, and what you truly are?

Rexon yawned and answered, *Exactly what I said. Good night, Ryuu. We need to rest now if we're going to get up early enough to leave unnoticed.*

You're right. Good night, Rexon. And with that, they went to bed, too tired to talk any further.

THE THIRD CHOSEN ONE

Early that next morning, Ryuu quietly got out of bed. *Rexon, wake up,* he called to Rexon with his thoughts. *We're going to go soon.*

Without lifting his head, Rexon yawned and opened his eyes. *Ryuu,* he said, *I've been thinking. Since we're going to leave in secret, shouldn't we gather as much provisions and supplies as possible? And another thing struck me too. You will need some new clothes.*

He was right. The clothes he was wearing were starting to smell. As a matter of fact, they were the only clothes he had now. *Right, let's go.*

Excited, Rexon leapt from where he was sleeping and flew onto Ryuu's shoulders. As quietly as he could, Ryuu crept down the hall. When they got to the stables, Ryuu grasped Arrolonn's reins and guided him out onto the crowded streets.

After several minutes had passed, Ryuu stepped into a shop that sold traveling clothes.

"Ah, good morning to you, m'lord. How may I help you?" asked the man behind the counter.

"Good morning to you too, sir. I'm looking for some clothes that can withstand a lot of traveling," Ryuu replied to the man.

"Oh, well then, you came to the right place!" said the man with glee. "Come this way if you please, m'lord. I think I have just the thing for you." The man led him into the back room where many different varieties of traveling clothes were hanging on clothes racks. "Now what kind of material are you looking for?" asked the tailor.

"Leather, if you have it."

"Oh, why of course I do. Just let me call my son. Kouri!" A few seconds later, a boy that looked just like the tailor came into the room.

"Yes, Father, what is it?" asked Kouri.

"Ah yes, good. Now can you please bring me some of the leather traveling clothes for me?"

"As you wish, Father." He turned around and headed into an upstairs room. As Kouri left, Ryuu's scar began to burn.

"That's a beautiful dragon. What's his name?" asked the man.

"Rexon, sir," Ryuu replied, feeling Rexon's lips curl into a smile on his shoulder.

"That's a good name. So milord, where are you from?" asked the man.

"What? Oh, I'm from ... uh—"
Garindel.
"Garindel, sir." *Thanks, Rexon.*

The man cocked an eyebrow. "Garindel, ay? Not too many people come from there these days, but no matter. Oh, by the way, I'm Vermorja."

He held out a hand for Ryuu to shake. "I'm Prince Ryuu. Pleased to meet you. Tell me, Vermorja, is your name an elvish name?"

Vermorja chuckled. "Why, of course it is. I'm surprised you even noticed. You see, my mother was an elf, and my father was a human. I got my dad's looks and my mother's ears and eyes, bless them. Anyway I was born in the elven capital, Synaigwa."

"It must be a beautiful place," said Ryuu.

"That it is. Now where is Kouri with those... ah, here he is."

Kouri reentered the room with a bundle of traveling clothes. Again Ryuu's scar burned. After Kouri put the clothes down, Ryuu noticed that he scratched his right wrist.

"Ah, why is it itching so much today?"

At that moment, Rexon jumped off Ryuu's shoulders and onto the pile of traveling clothes, lifted his wings, and was suddenly surrounded by icy blue flames,.

"What the heck is going on? Get away! Get away!" Kouri shrieked.

Before he could move, Rexon jabbed his head forward toward Kouri's chest. Kouri put his arms out in front of himself as if Rexon were going to bite him. "Huh? What the... oh." He fainted.

Ryuu rushed over to him and caught him before he fell over. "What on earth is going on?" bellowed Vermorja furiously.

Looking at Kouri's right wrist, Ryuu saw a scar with a dragon head surrounded by snowflakes that was glowing sapphire blue.

"What has your dragon done to my son? Well, *answer me!*" demanded Vermorja. Ryuu reached into the front of Kouri's shirt and pulled out a necklace. The pendant of the necklace was of a silver dragon with a sapphire gem between its wings. Ryuu knew what it was at once.

"Sir," he asked cautiously, "where did Kouri get this?"

Vermorja glared at Rexon for a while and then looked at Ryuu and said, "It's a family heirloom. I gave it to him on his fifteenth birthday last week as part of the family tradition. What of it?"

"Well, it's a Draggonian necklace, sir. You see, he's a chosen one."

Surprised at the news, Vermorja could barely speak. "He's a… He can't… Really? I never…"

Ryuu sighed. "Didn't you know about his scar?"

Clearly not hearing the question, Vermorja fell to his knees in shock. "A chosen one? So that's what it meant."

From this, Ryuu thought he knew about the scar on Kouri's right wrist. "He'll be up in about in an hour or so, so don't worry. He's just unconscious," Ryuu said reassuringly.

"Take… take whatever you like, no charge," said Vermorja.

"Vermorja!" bellowed Ryuu. "I will not leave here without paying you. Am I understood?"

Just then, two young men walked into the shop. One, Ryuu noticed, was a mage and the other a knight. The mage wore a black robe with a dark-blue trim. The symbol psi was upon his right breast, also sown with dark-blue thread. In his right hand was a six-foot-long staff. The last two feet of the staff was a silver blade with two medium-sized sapphire orbs in the middle of the blade. The knight wore shining white armor with a black trim. The symbol for fire was on his right shoulder guard. On his left hip was a sword. Tied around its wired wrapped hilt was a leather string that held on to two feathers. One was a Phoenix feather; the other was a great eagle feather.

"And as I said, Francis, I've heard it before. You told me the other day! Now you may be a mage, but your magic isn't stronger than mine. You need to stop reading those stupid spell books and get out more."

Francis the mage shook his head and argued back, "You and your opinions. You need to read more, Vincent. It's like I've said before. You—" He stopped midsentence and looked at Ryuu with slack-jawed wonder. "No, it can't be him. It just can't! It's like Christopher said, he does look like his father!"

GIFTS OF LEGEND

"Who are you?" asked Ryuu.

"You don't know us?" asked Francis. "Why, we're your cousins!"

Ryuu was bewildered. After all these years, he finally knew he had a living family.

"The truth is," Francis went on, "me and my brothers never thought we would ever see you, but considering the circumstances, I'm not surprised that we got to meet you."

"Circumstances? What circumstances?" asked Ryuu, surprised. Vincent laughed and pointed. Ryuu turned around to look at Kouri. "I see," he said, turning back to Vincent. "So why are you two here anyway?"

Vincent spoke up. "I came to pick up Kouri for his sword lessons, but now I'll have to wait for a while."

"You know," said Francis after a time, "I don't think you know any magic, do you, Ryuu?"

Ryuu shook his head. "No, I wasn't taught any spells."

Francis frowned. "Huh, that's going to complicate things a little."

Ryuu raised an eyebrow. "How so? And what do you mean?"

"Well," said Francis, "it's going to make it harder for you to learn how to use magic. If what you said is true and that you have no idea how to cast magic, then you're not going to leave this city until you know how magic works and how to use it properly!"

Ryuu winced. *How does he know that I'm planning to leave? It is as if he can read my mind.*

And that is exactly how I know, Ryuu. You also need to learn how to guard your mind better too.

Ryuu jumped to Francis's reply. He wasn't expecting that to happen.

"Also," added Vincent, "I would like to see how proficient you are with a sword."

"What about Kouri though?" asked Ryuu.

"Yes, what about my son?" Vermorja scowled. "I thought you were training him to become a hero?"

Vincent shook his head. "No, not a hero but a knight. Knights have to earn that title themselves. Once he's up and about again, the four of us will go to the practice fields. In the meantime, Francis, will you?"

Francis nodded, and from within his robes, he pulled out black robes and a black cloak that went with it. "This," he said, handing it to Ryuu, "is for you. It was Koichi's, but I think he would like you to have it."

Ryuu ran his fingers through the fabric. It felt smooth on his fingertips, like water. It also felt very light. "I don't know what to say. Thank you."

"This is also for you." From within his robes, Francis pulled out another item. Ryuu gasped at what Francis was holding. In his hands he held chained mythril armor.

"And this too," said Vincent, holding a mythril chest plate; mythril greaves, boots, shoulder pads, and gauntlets that were all painted silver and black with a gold trim; and a golden belt and crown-like helm.

"How the... Where the... Is this really...?" stuttered Ryuu, completely bewildered.

Francis raised a hand to silence him and answered Ryuu's unfinished questions in order. "First off, I used magic to shrink the size of the armor to make it easier to travel with. Having the armor pocket size made it easier to conceal from greedy eyes. It came from the city of magic, Trilindo. It's about twenty-four hundred miles from here to its west entrance, but that doesn't matter. Magic users, such as myself, and Dragon Knights can buy this armor at any armory there, but it's extremely expensive. You should count yourself lucky 'cause if it weren't for Christopher, you would have never been able to get your hands on one, especially a complete set. A complete set is worth a fortune. Mythril is hard to find these days though. All the known caves that had mythril crystals in them are now depleted. A long time ago it was legendary to even find some in a cave, but then more were found, and mining of the mineral began. But enough of the history lesson. Here you go."

Ryuu was speechless. He was amazed at how light the armor was. It was no heavier than a bundle of feathers. From upon his shoulders, Rexon looked at Francis, completely bewildered; even Vermorja seemed surprised and looked longingly at the armor in Ryuu's arms.

"I...I never thought I would see mythril armor. I don't know how to repay you. It's such a princely gift. Thank you," said Ryuu.

Francis threw back his head and laughed. "Well, Prince Ryuu, princely gifts should be given to the prince in question. Am I not right?" Laughing, Ryuu caught on to what Francis was laughing about and almost dropped the mythril armor.

"Now," said Vincent over the throng, sounding a little agitated but smiling nevertheless, "I think we should get going. Kouri seems to be coming about now. Ah, yes. Kouri, how do you feel?"

Kouri slowly lifted himself upright, completely confused. "F...fine I think. What happened?"

Vincent held out a hand to help him up, and Kouri took it appreciatively. "I'll explain everything on the way to the training fields. Come on now. Up you go. That's right. Rest a little. We'll be leaving soon."

"Say, Ryuu," said Vermorja.

"Yes?" asked Ryuu, cautiously.

"Why don't you try on your new armor? I have a changing room in the back. Why don't you use it for the time being while you wait to leave."

"Yeah, that's not a bad idea," said Ryuu. "Yeah, I think I'll do that. Thank you, Vermorja."

"I'll help," stated Vincent, and he followed Ryuu into the back of shop where the changing rooms were.

For a half hour, Vincent helped Ryuu into his new mythril armor. Tedious as it was, the armor was quite comfortable. Once everything was on, Ryuu put Koichi's old cloak on over his armor and joined the others in the front of the shop. Vermorja and Kouri looked at him in awe.

"Now there's a prince of Garindel," announced Vermorja. "Should we bow to you in your presence?"

Ryuu laughed. "No, there's no need for that. So how do I look?"

"Very royal," commented Francis. "Now, let's get going before the training fields get filled up." They hailed Vermorja farewell, thanked him for his time, and left for the practice fields.

OF SWORDPLAY AND CASTING MAGIC

It took them nearly fifteen minutes to get to the training fields. Ryuu saw men in thick, heavy armor. They held foot-wide swords in one hand and a thick, heavy shield in the other. Ryuu pointed them out to Vincent, who nodded.

"They're Guardians, elite warriors. They are the most feared soldiers next to the Dragon Knights." They watched them for a time before moving on. Ryuu was surprised by how fast they were in their heavy, iron-clad armor. Their swords were so strong and heavy that their blows could knock down any regular foot soldier, destroy regular swords, shatter a normal shield, and cut through any armor. Ryuu asked if any Guardians had been defeated by regular soldiers before.

Vincent shook his head. "No. They may look easy to overwhelm, but nothing can penetrate their armor." Ryuu noticed open areas in the armor and noted to himself to go for those points if he ever had to take one down. Walking over to an open area of the field, Vincent took Kouri to practice swordplay, and Francis took Ryuu to educate him in the use of magic.

"Now," he said, "the first thing you need to know is that magic should only be used as a last resort. In battle, your energy will be drained, and it will be harder to use magic."

"Energy?" Ryuu interrupted.

Francis nodded. "Yes, energy. Energy that is stored in your amulet is used to fuel the magic you cast. Most magic will take the same amount of energy to complete its task if you were to do it the mundane way. Some spells are more complex and require more energy to be cast. If you cast spells you're not ready for, it will kill you or leave you unconscious for several hours."

Ryuu thought over what Francis had said, then asked, "What if I desperately need to use a spell in the middle of a battle? Would it weaken me so much that I would die anyway?" asked Ryuu.

Francis nodded again. "Yes, that could happen, if you were a regular spell caster. The more you grow up, the less energy you will lose. The more you practice with magic, the stronger you'll get. Take me for example. I've used magic for years now, and I can constantly cast spells that are powerful without even feeling weary."

"So," said Ryuu, "strength and power comes with age?"

Francis nodded for a third time.

"So how do I summon the energy to use magic?" asked Ryuu. Francis closed his eyes in thought, thinking on how to best answer his question.

After a moment, Rexon said, *Dragon Knight magic is considered to be of a different nature to ordinary spell users due to the fact that their necklace gives them their magical powers. Am I not right, Francis?*

Francis looked at him, amazed. "How do you... But of course, you activate that power when you touch the gem on their necklace. And of course you know that. You've lived for over a hundred years now."

Well, said Rexon, *I'm a hundred and fifty two to be exact.*

"Well, anyway, Ryuu," continued Francis, "I'm not sure how to tell you how to use your magic properly, but I can teach you the basics. Vincent can tell you more on how to use your magic since he's already had this kind of experience. But in any case, let us begin. Now, I need you to close your eyes. Now look through your thoughts and find a memory that is dear to you and draw strength from it."

Ryuu didn't need to look for long, for the memory that was dearest to him popped into his mind without effort. "All right, what do I do next?"

Francis came up to Ryuu and whispered into his ear, "On the count of three, I want you to say the word *bratiego* aloud. Nod to me when you are ready." Ryuu nodded. "All right, one, two, three, *now!*"

Raising his right hand, Ryuu bellowed, "*Bratiego!*" A jet of silver flames erupted from the center of his hand, scorching the ground. For a moment, everything went silent but for the flames billowing from Ryuu's hand. Then a yell of agony pierced the silence, and the flames died down. It took Ryuu a moment to realize that he was the one who screamed and that he was on his hands and knees.

"Ryuu, how do you feel?" asked Francis, crouching down to put a comforting hand on Ryuu's back.

"Terrible." He gasped, surprised of how weak he felt.

"Maybe that spell was too much for you to handle. Here. I'll give you some of my strength to steady yourself." Ryuu felt a flow of energy run through his body. A moment later, he felt his limbs relax. Standing up again, he readied himself for a different spell.

"Here, give me your hand," said Francis. Ryuu gave him his left hand, and without warning, Francis ran a razor sharp knife over his palm, drawing blood. Cursing, Ryuu grasped his bleeding hand.

"What was that for?"

"Be quiet, and I'll tell you," said Francis sharply. Ryuu fell silent and listened. "Now say the word *healria'oeso*. I know it's a bit of a tongue twister, so say it a few times to practice saying the word if you need to. By the way, what memory did you use?" Ryuu looked at him, surprised. "You don't have to tell me if you don't want to. Most of our dearest memories are the most personal ones."

Ryuu nodded in agreement. "That is true, but if you haven't noticed, I think you just killed my hand."

Francis laughed. "Well, I believe we should do something about that. Try using the spell I just gave you."

Gathering his strength, Ryuu dove into the magic and bellowed the spell, "*Healria'oeso!*" But nothing happened. The wound on Ryuu's left hand was *gone*. There was no trace of a scar.

Francis frowned. "That's odd. The wound was suppose to glow, but how could it have healed before you cast the spell?"

Ryuu shrugged then started panting heavily. Even though the spell didn't do anything, his whole body was shaking from the effort of using the spell. "That took more energy than I thought. Even that spell left me tired."

Francis nodded. "Yes, it did, but that might be because of the spell you used before that one left you tired and weakened from its cost of energy. But you mastered the basics with very little effort. That's enough to convince me that you can use magic. Well done. Now before you start sparring with Vincent, there are—"

"Those were the basics?" interrupted Ryuu. "Those were pretty advanced spells for the basics, don't you think?"

Francis laughed. "The spells were advanced, yes, but necessary because it showed me how much you could handle. Also, the spells used in basic training don't really matter because I was teaching you how to summon magic. Now, Rexon, if you will restore the energy in Ryuu's amulet for me, there are some other spells you'll need to know for your journey, Ryuu. Now let us begin."

Ryuu listened very carefully to what Francis was saying. Francis gave him a variety of new spells to remember for when he was on the road. *Friega,* a weaker fire spell than *bratiego,* but strong enough to start a campfire and cause minor injuries. *Lil'tia,* a spell for casting a small ball of light to light up dark places. *Amtrie,* a spell for hunting with a bow and arrow with bull's eye accuracy. And *Shyrie,* to cast a protective barrier around your body to avoid injury in battle. He also gave Ryuu a spell to read other's minds without detection, called *redga.* After that, they watched Vincent and Kouri with their swordplay. Vincent occasionally stopped the fight to give Kouri tips and to teach him new attacks to practice.

They sparred for another half an hour before stopping and swapping students, Francis with Kouri and Vincent with Ryuu. "Now then," said Vincent, "how do you fight with a sword? Do you fight edge on edge, or do fight with the flat of the blade?"

Ryuu thought for a moment, trying to recall how he fought Mávro Dráko a week ago. "Well," said Ryuu, "I think it was edge on edge, but I'm not sure. Come to think of it, I think I also fought backhanded."

Vincent raised an eyebrow. "That's interesting. Not too many people fight backhanded with a sword that has a cross guard. Elven swords are easier to use when fighting backhanded, for their curved blades don't have cross guards. Christopher also fights like that when he's not using his Guardian sword. Well, in any case, let us begin. Come. Show me what you're made of!"

Readying himself, Vincent held his ivory-colored sword up in front of himself. Wanting to make a good first impression, Ryuu drew Destiny from its sheath and held it backhanded like before. Vincent's eyes widened at the sight of the golden blade. The entire training field went silent, and everyone's head turned to look at him holding the ancient sword in his hand.

"So then," said Vincent in a soft voice, "Voggna is dead?"

Ryuu nodded and prepared to fight.

It was an incredible duel. Ryuu and Vincent fought for hours without rest; neither one of them showed signs of weakness. Neither one of them could touch the other either. No matter how hard one tried, they didn't let the other land a blow. Eventually Vincent tried to end the duel with a quick maneuver, but before he could do so, Ryuu, feeling very tired, drew his other sword from its sheath and held the tip of the blade to his neck, stopping him in place.

"Dead," said Ryuu cooly.

"Dead," agreed Vincent.

"That...that was amazing!" exclaimed Kouri. "None of my duels were that intense! I kept expecting one of you to injure the other, but then the other would block and parry. It just kept going on and on and on..." He went on like that for a time, naming every move from their duel even after they left the practice field.

You did well, Ryuu.

Ryuu jumped, hearing the words in his head. *Oh, thank you, Rexon,* he said with his thoughts. *I'm sorry that I forgot about you. Where did you go after my magic lessons?*

Well, said Rexon, landing on Arrolonn's saddle, *I watched you from Arrolonn's back for a time; then I got dis-*

tracted by a silver phoenix that perched itself on a nearby spire.

Ryuu looked at him in surprise. *A silver phoenix? I've never heard of such a creature. Where do they come from?*

Rexon cocked his head in thought and then said, *Most phoenixes come from the Phoenix Plain just north of where Voggna's temple was, but this one came from the Twilight Mountains northeast of here.*

Ryuu looked back at him, confused. *The Twilight Mountains?* he asked. *Don't you mean the Mythril Mountains?*

Rexon shook his head. *No, I mean the Twilight Mountains. I'll tell you more later. But as I was saying before, it looked at me as if it was waiting for me, so I flew over to him. We talked for a while before he flew off into the sky. By that time, you were in the middle of your duel, so I watched from on top the spire.*

Ryuu yawned, tired from his duel with Vincent. *So after that you came down when we left the fields right?* Rexon nodded and fell asleep on Arrolonn's back.

Suddenly a loud horn echoed throughout the city. Vincent, Francis, Kouri, and the people in the streets froze with fear. Rexon lifted his head and immediately jumped off Arrolonn's back and flew toward the Great Hall, as if he were waiting for that signal

"No, not now!" said Vincent, clearly terrified by the noise.

"What?" asked Ryuu.

"That horn is only blown when the enemy approaches," answered Francis. "If they are near, they will—" But he was cut off by another blow on the horn. Francis closed his eyes.

"Blow the horn a second time," said Ryuu, finishing Francis's sentence. He nodded.

"They'll need me at the gate! Vincent, take Kouri home! Ryuu, warn the royal family. They need to be protected!" Ryuu and Vincent nodded. "Then go! Make haste!" Ryuu jumped on his horse and sped off down the street, following the path Rexon took to the Great Hall.

ESCAPE FROM OAKWIN

"Out of the way! Out of the way!" Ryuu bellowed as he charged through the panicking crowd. The city was in utter chaos as huge flaming boulders came crashing down on the city. Mothers were grabbing their children; people were pushing each other out of their way and falling over each other as they ran for safety. Ryuu felt it might be safer for him to find the nearest ally to gallop through instead of through the streets to avoid trampling someone on accident. He found an alley that would lead him right to the Great Hall and went charging through it.

As he rounded the corner, an ear-piercing shriek came from behind him. He spun around in his saddle to find a black-cloaked figure charging toward him, dragging a black-bladed sword with dark purple edges along the ground, creating a deep cut in the stone street. Arrolonn panicked and reared, throwing Ryuu off the saddle, and bolted. But as Ryuu fell, his wrist got caught on Arrolonn's reins, and he was being dragged alongside the frightened horse on the stone pavement.

"Oh, come on!" he yelled at the horse, "I just got these robes! They were Koichi's! You're ruining them, you stupid horse!" Drawing his dagger from him belt, he slashed at the reins, cutting himself free.

"Watch out, milord!" A group of three Guardians came from behind him, charging at the cloaked stranger that was chasing him. Suddenly, the thing dove forward and went straight through the ground. The Guardians skidded to a halt and looked around in confusion, their swords raised high above their heads. Without warning, the thing leapt out of the ground right in front of the Guardian in the middle of their formation, making a backhanded, upwards slash with its sword. The Guardian fell backward, dead; a wide gash ran up the middle of his armor up to his neck. However, when the thing made its upper cut, it rose into the air. It turned around and came down on one of the other Guardians with unnatural speed. The man howled in agony and fell, dead; a wide gash ran along his side. Then for the last time, the thing moved toward the last Guardian with another burst of unnatural speed, its hand out stretched. Suddenly, the Guardian was thrown off his feet and was hurled against a wall with an unseen force. He rebounded off the wall, and before he could even fall to the ground, the thing stabbed its sword through his chest, pinning him to the wall. His head went limp, and he died. "No!" bellowed Ryuu, but he realized that he had made a mistake in saying this, for the thing's attention was redirected back to him again. The thing drew its sword out of the man's body and slung it across its back. Then the thing did something Ryuu was not expecting. It crouched down on all fours and bounded toward him like some animal. As the thing charged at him, black, swirling smoke surrounded it, and it turned into a big black wolf. Ryuu was frozen to the spot. He tried to move, but his body seemed to refuse to do his will. As soon as the black wolf was almost upon him, it made a great leap to pounce on him. But before the wolf could land on him, a flash of silver jolted toward the wolf, hitting it from its side, and Ryuu watched the wolf being hurled to the opposite side of the street.

"Are you all right, son?"

Ryuu turned to look at the person who spoke, but the voice did not come from a man but from a silver wolf with strange markings on it.

"Silver Tail?" he asked.

The wolf nodded. "That isn't my real name, actually" said the wolf. "My actual name is Tarin, and I've been watching over you, my son." Ryuu got to his feet and backed away, not believing a word he was hearing.

"You can't be Tarin, and if you are, why did you rescue me?"

Silver Tail raised an eyebrow. "Did you not just hear me, Ryuu? Why would I let my only son die?" He said this with so much affection. Ryuu could not believe a word he was hearing.

"You're lying," he said, shaking his head. "Koichi's my father, not you."

Silver Tail shook his head. "So that's what they've been telling you all these years," he said more to himself than to Ryuu. "Koichi is not your father, Ryuu. He was your guardian, your uncle. You see, I…" He paused and then shook his head again. "No, this isn't the time and place for the full story. Right now we need to get to the Great Hall."

Ryuu raised an eyebrow, "We?" he asked.

Silver Tail nodded. "Aye, we. You're going to need all the help you can get now that the *eight* are abroad again. I haven't seen you in years, Fenrir. Pity you didn't fade when my brother Cyndrio gave his life to save us all." He directed his last words toward the black wolf that was unconscious on the other side of the street.

"Who…what is Fenrir?" asked Ryuu, shaken at the memory of moments before when the dark-cloaked figure turned into the black wolf that just tried to pounce on him.

"I can't tell you everything now," said Silver Tail, "but know this of him: he is a Shadow Lord." And with that, he beckoned Ryuu to follow him. Ryuu did so and drew his sword, Destiny, from its sheath. They trotted along the street to the Great Hall where Rexon was waiting for them, along with the queen and princesses on their horses, and among them was a man who looked strangely familiar.

"Christopher?" asked Ryuu, completely bewildered.

The man nodded, then said, "Good, you found him, Tarin." Ryuu looked at Silver Tail and then at Christopher, puzzled. "Look," said Christopher, "I know you have many questions for me, but as I told the others, I'll answer your questions later. Now's not the time for gossip. We must fly from this place. It is too dangerous for you and the others to be here. We ride to Evevana, one of Oakwin's coastal cities, where a ship is waiting for us to take us to the elves. Sir Vincent has agreed to meet us there with Kouri. Now, onward!"

"Wait!" said Ryuu.

"What, Ryuu?" asked Christopher, a little annoyed. "We cannot linger."

Ryuu looked at him, noticing that his voice had a hint of fear in it, and then asked, "Did any of you see Arrolonn pass by here?"

Christopher nodded and then frowned. "He went past here not too long ago. I tried calling him, but he kept running away."

Ryuu groaned. "What am I supposed to do now?" he asked.

Christopher sighed, contemplated the situation, and said with the utmost regret, "I had hoped that this wouldn't have to come to this, but you'll need the experience. Tarin, will you do the honors?"

Silver Tail nodded, rose up into the air, and started to glow. Ryuu gaped at the wolf, but it wasn't a wolf anymore. No, it was a great silver dragon with the same black and gold symbols that ran down its back. The dragon had four black horns that all protruded backward. A little bit of white hair grew out from underneath his chin, and it had sapphire eyes, Ryuu's eyes.

"Everyone," said Christopher, "let me introduce you to my lifelong friend, Tarin Twilight, a Twilight Dragon."

The dragon bowed and said, "Ryuu, my son, I'll be your steed for the time being. Once you have a full-grown dragon of your own, you'll have the experience of riding dragon back. Unfortunately, we do not have time to fit me into a saddle, so you'll have to ride me bare back."

Ryuu nodded and climbed up Tarin's right foreleg with a little difficulty. Tarin swung his head around to help him up. "Tarin," said Christopher concerned, "you can fly ahead of us and meet us at the ship if you want to."

Tarin shook his head. "No," he said, "I'm taking him straight to them."

With the realization of what Tarin was about to do, Christopher yelled, "Tarin, no!" But it was too late. Tarin had bounded down the street and leapt into the air.

Ryuu held on to Tarin's neck for dear life. They rose higher and higher as Tarin turned toward the east. "Where are we going?" asked Ryuu over the torrent of wind.

"To Ashryno Forest, where the elves live," said Tarin over his shoulder.

"How far away is it?" asked Ryuu. Tarin cocked his head in thought and then answered, "I believe it will take us the rest of the day to get halfway there."

As they flew on, Ryuu kept looking over his shoulder, fearing that they were being pursued by Fenrir. "Why haven't we been followed, Tarin?" he asked after a while.

Tarin looked over his shoulder at him; a fearful expression was on his face. "I don't know," he said, turning his head back around to face forward. "I'm starting to worry about that too."

They didn't speak for several minutes, neither of them wanting to say what was on their minds. Ryuu wondered what happened to the others; he was worried about them. What fate had befallen them? As if Tarin was reading his mind, he said, "I don't know, Ryuu. Christopher is with them, so they should be all right."

Ryuu nodded in agreement and yawned. Tarin looked at him and smiled, then slowly began to descend. "Tarin?" asked Ryuu.

"Yes?"

"What is that thing up ahead?" He pointed toward a massive object in the distance that seemed to shimmer in the early twilight.

"That," said Tarin sorrowfully, "is the Vera Tree. I'll tell you more when we get there." He drifted down toward the Vera Tree on silent wings.

As they got closer, Ryuu realized how big the tree was getting. The tree's trunk and branches were iridescent silver, and all its leaves were the color of pure gold. The tree was bigger than anything Ryuu had ever seen apart from Cyndrio Tower.

"How big is this tree?" he asked, amazed at its gigantic size.

"Well," said Tarin thoughtfully, "I've really never thought about it before, but I would have to guess at least three miles high. In any case, we're stopping here for the night."

As they landed next to the tree, Ryuu gazed up its trunk. He jumped off Tarin's back and walked closer to the tree. His neck started to hurt from looking up so long. Lowering his head to look at the base of the trunk, he noticed that something was etched in the bark. He moved forward to look closer. The etchings turned out to be a carving of a heart with two names engraved on the inside of it that read *Tarin and Vera*. Words were also written underneath the heart that read, *For you and my family, my heart will be pure and always shall be.* Then underneath those words, something else was written in a language Ryuu had never seen before.

Suddenly, a flash of light blazed behind him. He whirled around, ready to fight, but the flash of light turned out to only be Tarin changing his form again. Ryuu recoiled. Kneeling before him wasn't a dragon but a man with his head bowed, his black hair obscuring his face. Tarin stood up and flipped back his hair to reveal his countenance. Ryuu gasped and fell to his knees in shock. Tarin was a mirror image of himself, only he was older. His hair was longer, running down toward to the middle of his back. They both had the same sapphire eyes and the same lightly tanned skin too. Without a doubt, Ryuu realized who this man was. He had known it from the very moment he saved his life and named him his son.

"Father?" he asked, tears filling his eyes.

Tarin nodded and walked over to him and said, "It's time you learned about your true legacy, Ryuu. Too long have you been in shadow. Too long have you been lied to. Your life has been nothing but a lie until tonight!

Tonight, you'll get the whole truth. Tonight, you'll finally understand what you truly are. Hear me out, my son. Ask me a question, and I'll give you an answer, for the truth lies with me. Hear me out, son, and know all that has been kept from you."

Ryuu shuddered; there was so much he wanted to know, yet he didn't know which question he should ask first. Making up his mind, he asked in a shaky voice, "Why did you abandon me?"

Tarin knelt beside him and answered, "I did not abandon you, Ryuu. I protected you. I wish it didn't have to come to this, but—" He broke off and shook his head. "This might take me awhile to answer you fully. Let me make a fire and find something to eat for the both of us. It won't take me long, but when I get back, I promise you I'll answer your question. I need some time to think." He stood up and began to walk away, but he stopped and turned to Ryuu and said, "Stay close to the tree. The power of twilight lingers here. The enemy will never come near it. They fear that power, and I believe that my presence has frightened them as well." And with that, he changed his form back into a dragon and flew off, leaving Ryuu alone by the great Vera Tree.

THE TRUTH

Tarin returned with a wild buck he had caught, laid the dead animal next to the firewood he gathered earlier, and set to work on making a pit for the fire. Using his massive claws, they had a decent fire pit within minutes. With that done, Tarin turned back into a human and began to skin the buck, leaving Ryuu start the fire. Ryuu gathered the firewood and arranged them so that they stood on end and leaned against each other. He then stooped down and concentrated his thoughts on the kindling under the logs. Reaching for the power that resided in his amulet, he whispered, "Friega," and flames came to life. Soon they had a roaring fire. Ryuu watched it for a time in case it should falter. Deciding that it would stay ablaze, he stood up and walked over to Tarin to help him finish carving the meat. They worked in silence, neither making a sound. Ryuu looked at Tarin's face. His expression was full of concentration as he cut the meat into small strips. Ryuu could tell that Tarin was still thinking how to answer his questions, so he waited patiently and didn't disturb his thoughts. When the meat was ready for cooking, they fried the strips on slabs of rock that they found near by the clearing, seasoned them to their liking with plants from the surrounding area, and ate in silence. When they finished eating, Tarin finally spoke.

"Now, I know that you must have several questions for me, but I shall answer what you first asked me. Why did I abandon you? The night you were taken to Voggna's temple, I was summoned to the Council of Dragon Elders to discuss a serious matter that had arisen. There had been reports that our ancient foes were abroad again and that they were growing in power. These foes I speak of are the ones who attacked Oakwin today, the Shadow Lords. You've already met three of them, Mávro Dráko, Fenrir, and Ivinrah. Mávro Dráko is the youngest among their ranks and is the one who destroyed Master Voggna's temple and the one you've already fought. Ivinrah revealed himself the night Garindel City was destroyed. There was nothing I could do when I was so far away, but your mother and I had been planning just for this kind of event. We arranged for Dragon Master Koichi to take you away from the city to keep you safe, for we feared that you might very well be Ivinrah's target. We wanted to hide you from the Shadow Lords and to keep you a secret from the world. I never went looking for you, so yes, I *did* abandon you. Not until recently did I start looking for you. I wanted to make sure it was safe to do so. I have watched over you for ten whole years. At night, I would disguise myself as a silver wolf and climb in through your open bedroom window and curl up beside your bed and leave right before the dawn."

"That was *you*? I remember having a dream about a silver wolf that came into my room and sat down next to my bed, leaving at dawn."

Tarin nodded. "Yes, there was a night that you saw me, but you were so tired you couldn't make heads or tails of it."

Ryuu smiled.

"Why do you smile?" asked Tarin.

"It's nothing really. I just remembered something. When I saw you in my room, didn't I ask you if it was a dream, and you nodded?"

Tarin laughed. Ryuu took joy in hearing him laugh; it was the same as his. "Yes," said Tarin, "I remember that. I believe you fell asleep after that and woke up just before I left too."

"Tarin?"

"Yes, Ryuu?"

"Who was my mother? What was she like?"

Tarin frowned, apparently unsettled by the question. "Your mother? Well, she loved everything to do with nature. She sang to the trees and to the flowers. She loved to dance among the fairies at night and listen to their sweet melodies. She loved climbing into the trees and singing with the birds. She loved to lie in the grass and watch the clouds go by overhead. She knew how to make me happy when I was upset. She would always hum the sweetest melodies that made you forget about all else but the melody. She was always kind to the unfortunate, and she was always willing to help an injured animal, no matter how dangerous it was."

"You speak of her as if she was an elf," Ryuu interjected.

Tarin nodded. "Yes, she was an elf."

Ryuu's eyes widened. "What was her name, and what did she look like?" he asked.

"Well," said Tarin, "her name was Emily, and she was beautiful. She had long, wavy brown hair that shone in the sun and rippled like water in the wind. She had dazzling brown eyes and rosy cheeks. Her smile was as bright as the sun, and her sweet voice seemed to always be in song."

Then Ryuu asked, "If what you say is true, and you really are my father, does that make me a dragon too, but only in human form?"

Tarin looked at him thoughtfully and said, "I'm not sure, Ryuu. Has there ever been something you did that you could never explain?"

"There is something I can't make heads or tails of."

Tarin raised an eyebrow. "Oh? And what may that be?"

"Every time I look at my reflection, I always see a silver dragon, and when I blink, the dragon is gone and I see myself in its place. And there's something Rexon told me a few weeks ago. He said, 'Deep within your heart, you know who and what you truly are.' I couldn't make heads or tails of that either. Do you have an idea of what he was talking about?"

Tarin nodded. "Yes, that makes everything clear to me now. You *are* a dragon but in human form. I don't know if you'll have great powers like me, but I do know that if my blood runs through your veins, then it has the same magical abilities as mine."

"What's so magical about your blood?" interrupted Ryuu, eager to know the answer.

"I thought you might ask me that. You see, normal dragon blood is magical, but Twilight Dragon blood is different. If you drink Twilight Dragon blood, you become immune to all disease and pain and are given long life, making you immortal. But bathe in it, and you become invulnerable to attacks. Making you invincible. Christopher is a living example of this."

"Christopher?" said Ryuu, disbelieving.

Tarin nodded. "When he was young, I believe right around your age, he was forced to drink and bathe in a Twilight Dragon's blood by Ivinrah on Lord Vozlin's orders."

Ryuu looked at his father, puzzled. "Lord Vozlin's orders? Who's he?"

"The Dark Lord of Shadows. His real name was Cyndrio. He once was the king of the dragon race. My parents named my eldest brother after him. He's also my great ancestor."

"You said that Vozlin was once your king. What happened to him?"

"You see, Vozlin traveled to the dark lands known as Darkensoan and fell to the darkness there. That was over four thousand years ago. Vozlin disappeared for over a thousand years before he returned for the first time. I still remember the first time I met him. He looked exactly like my brother Cyndrio, except his eyes were emerald, not sapphire like my brother's and mine."

"Who's Ivinrah?" asked Ryuu.

"He's one of the eight Shadow Lords, but there's something different about him. His powers are stronger; his body is nothing but twisted shadows, not of flesh and bone like the rest. The other six are dragons that have fallen to the darkness, and Mávro Dráko is like Ivinrah, but he has flesh and bones."

"What are the other six Shadow Lords' names?" Ryuu interrupted.

"You know three names already, but I'll tell you all of them. They are Ivinrah, the Living Shadow; Mávro Dráko , the Angel of Darkness; Fenrir, the Dark Wolf; Grivenvor, the Dark Eclipse; Vermorsinja, the Black Fang; Shade, the Hell Riser; Damorzore, the Dark Rider; and Orphious, the Death Bringer. Now as I was saying before about your blood, if it's like mine, then your injuries will heal faster than usual. If you broke one of your bones right now, it would heal within a few minutes. Another thing, your blood is dangerous to all others but dragons and divine creatures. Don't ever share your blood, even if it were to save someone's life. Look at Christopher. Look at what happened to him; he should have died ages ago, but he didn't because of the blood."

Suddenly, a small ball of fire flew toward the two of them. Ryuu dived aside and drew his dagger. But the flame just stopped in front of Tarin's face and floated there for a while. Tarin kept his gaze upon the little flame with concentration until it faded away. "What *was* that?" asked Ryuu, bewildered.

"A Phoenix Call," replied Tarin.

"A what?"

"A *Phoenix Call*. It's a spell to send a message directly to the person who's supposed to receive it. Christopher just sent me a message. He said that he and the others got to the ship safely and that they are now sailing to the elves and will be there in three days' time."

Ryuu sighed with relief; they were safe. He had been worrying about Elizabeth and the others ever since he left them. "We should get some sleep," said Tarin. "You can ask me more questions tomorrow. I am tired, and you look so as well. I'll take the first watch."

Ryuu nodded and went to sleep. The last thing he saw before he went to sleep was his father changing back into a dragon.

AN UNEASY DECISION

Christopher stood upon the deck of the *Rehnorrin*, the ship that would take him and the others to the elves in Haidose. They barely made it to the ship alive, for three of the Shadow Lords chased them from Oakwin. It took all of his strength to fight them off, even with Sir Vincent at his side. He sighed, wondering where Tarin and Ryuu were now. He looked up into the sky that was threatening them with rain.

"Well, at least we're safe for now," he muttered to himself. Moments later, Vincent came up from below decks with his left arm wrapped in bandages, but the cloth was heavily stained with his blood. "How are you?" Christopher asked him once he was in ear shot.

"Tired" was all he said when he got to his side.

"How bad was the wound?"

Vincent just shrugged. "I really don't know, but if I was someone else, the blow would have been fatal. A wound inflicted by a Shadow Lord takes a long time to heal fully on its own."

Christopher eyed him wearily. "Why don't you let Rexon heal that for you?" he asked, eyeing Vincent's bandages.

"Because," said Vincent, wincing a little and gripping his arm, "he's busy healing Cassea with Francis down below. She's not doing well. Her injuries won't heal properly."

Christopher looked at him gravely. If Rexon's healing powers weren't working and if Francis's magic wasn't helping either, then they would have to fear the worst. Hours before they boarded the ship, the Shadow Lord Fenrir pounced on Cassea and bit her viciously. If Vincent didn't intervene, she would have been dead within seconds.

"I'll go help," he announced and then left Vincent's side to go below decks with one thing on his mind. "*I have no choice but to.*"

The door to Cassea's room stood ajar. Christopher stared at the door hesitantly, not wanting to see what was inside. He closed his eyes; memories of his past flashed through his mind, memories he had not recalled for years. Images of his wife and daughter came into his thoughts, and he shook his head to rid himself of them.

Pull yourself together, Christopher. Now's not the time to brood over the past. What happened, happened. There's nothing you can do now, but this should be recompense enough for them, I hope.

With renewed confidence, he entered the room. Francis sat next to Cassea and held her hand in his.

Rexon sat beside her head on the pillows and gazed at her face with sorrow in his eyes. Francis looked up at him with a grim expression and shook his head. Trembling, Christopher strolled over to Cassea's cot and looked upon her figure. Vincent was right; she didn't look good. She lay there as one dead, pale as a ghost. Her breathing was shallow and slow. He knelt down beside her and touched her hand. He jump back and wrenched his hand back away from her, shocked by how cold she was. Rexon laid his head on Cassea's shoulder and whimpered. Francis stood up without spoken consent and put a hand on Christopher's shoulder and then left the room and closed the door.

Christopher heard voices on the other side of the door and knew it was Francis telling the others the unfortunate news. Christopher shook his head and made up his mind; he was going to do what he felt was right. "*Lithriah,*" he muttered, and the door behind him suddenly locked itself.

Rexon lifted his head and looked at him gravely. *What are you going to do, Christopher?* he asked him.

Christopher only shook his head. "I don't know anymore, Rexon. I have no choice but to." With that, he drew his knife from his belt and pressed the blade's edge onto his palm. Beads of blood trickled down the knife as he made the incision. Satisfied, he drew the blade away from his hand. Where there should have been a deep cut in his palm was only unmarked skin. No evidence remained to show that he had just cut himself but for the blood on his knife.

Are you sure of this, Christopher? asked Rexon, concerned. Christopher shook his head and wiped the blood off the blade onto Cassea's lips. "If this doesn't work," he whispered, "then I don't know what will." Then he unlocked the door, left the room, and went back above decks to the cool night air.

A FAMILIAR FACE FROM LONG AGO

Christopher stood upon the *Rehnorrin's* deck once more, going over what he had just done.

"You know, you made a very risky choice there," said a voice from behind him. Christopher spun around. Leaning against the mizzenmast of the ship was a man with a black and red phoenix on his shoulder. The man wore a crimson tunic with black armor. His hair was long like Christopher's, only his was ginger. His head was bowed, and his hair obscured his face. A sword, very much like Christopher's Guardian blade, except that it had crimson-colored edges to its blade, was slung across his back.

"Who are you?" demanded Christopher, reaching for his sword.

"Have you honestly forgotten your old friend's face?" Lifting his head, the stranger took one of his hands and brushed away the hair that concealed his countenance.

Christopher turned pale and took a step back in shock. He knew the man who was before him. He remembered him from his childhood. They had grown up as farm boys together in Synaio Valley in the village Evelan. Memories—sweet, bitter memories—went through his mind, and he remembered his name and remembered that the last time he saw his brother-in-law was over three thousand years ago.

"You're dead, Ifirris," was all that Christopher managed to say. Ifirris raised one of his thin eyebrows, surprised by Christopher's sudden hostility.

Then he said, "You're right. By all means, I should be dead, but I can explain. You see, after our home was destroyed by the great black dragon Grivenvor, I swore an oath to kill him. When I turned eighteen and was strong and fit, I began my hunt for revenge. When I left Synaio Valley, I told my sister Molly that if I ever saw you I would let her know how you were as soon as I could. She was worried sick about you. You left and never returned, and when you did, our village had been burned to the ground and she—"

"That's enough!" bellowed Christopher, grabbing his sword and pointing it at Ifirris's chest, tears pouring down his cheeks. He did not want to remember that memory of Molly. He did not want to remember how his wife died in his arms, how he could have saved her if he had the power to do so.

Ifirris looked down, ashamed. "I'm sorry," he said. "I forgot how much you loved her."

They stood there in silence. After a while, Christopher lowered his sword and slung it across his back. Ifirris lifted his head and looked at him.

"You know what I did to myself, right, Christopher?"

Christopher nodded. He knew all right; he knew very well indeed. Ifirris had drunk the blood of the same dragon he had been forced to drink and bathe in by Ivinrah so long ago.

"Storm's coming soon," said Christopher. "We should get below deck before it starts. We have a lot to talk about."

Ifirris nodded in agreement and followed his brother-in-law back below deck. As soon as Ifirris went down the first step, lightning flashed and crackled in the sky and the thunder began to roar, and very suddenly, it began to rain so heavily that it looked like the ship was traveling through a great waterfall. Christopher quickly climbed back up the stairs and closed the trapdoor and thought one thing as he glimpsed the pounding rain. *We'll be lucky enough to get through the night at this rate. I've condemned everyone to their doom.*

RIVER OF CIDER

Ryuu woke to a beautiful sunny morning under the Vera Tree. Looking around, he noticed that Tarin was gone. Panicking, he stood up and began to search for his father. He was nowhere to be found. Out of desperation, he called Tarin's name. Then a voice in his head said, *Do not worry. I'm off hunting. Give me a few minutes.*

Ryuu sighed and said with his thoughts, *You can speak telepathically too?*

Yes, I can if I want.

Ryuu chuckled to himself. *Leave me a note or a message next time, okay?*

Tarin gave him an acknowledgment and left Ryuu's thoughts. Sighing, Ryuu went over to the fire that he made last night. The flames had almost died down, and now it was nothing but a smoldering mound of charcoal, but it was still hot enough to cook breakfast. As he ate, he watched the wildlife around him. He saw drófonns - creatures that looked like a mixture of a lion and a wolf with horns climbing the mountainsides, draiphmores, a relative to deer, but their horns were more exotic and were long, thick, and flat and went strait back like a dragon's. They had claws instead of hooves, and their fur coats were longer, and they were grazing the grass in the plains of Spirit Field. Exotic birds flew through the sky, wolves and their packs hunted deer across the plains, and wild horses galloped by, tossing their heads gracefully in the wind. Just from seeing how normal everything was made the past few days seem nothing more than a dream to Ryuu. Drawing Destiny from its sheath, he examined the golden blade and black inscription. It was the same strange language that was inscribed on the tree! He made a mental note to himself to ask Tarin what the language was and what both inscriptions read.

Suddenly, the sky around the Vera Tree went black, making everything seem nothing more than strange figures in shadow. *Father!* Ryuu called out with his thoughts. He did not know what was going on, but he had a strange feeling that something unearthly was watching him. He spun around to look toward the forest nearby. Then, two dark-crimson eyes appeared on the edge of the forest and gazed directly at Ryuu. The crimson eyes squinted, and Ryuu heard words of power emanate from the thing in the shadows. With a yelp, Ryuu dropped Destiny; the sword suddenly burned white hot. Before the sword even landed on the ground, it shattered into a million tiny pieces. Suddenly, a great ravenous roar filled the air. A silver shadow ran across the ground, and Tarin burst out of the ground like Lord Fenrir did when he killed the Guardians. With a tremendous growl, he shot a great beam of light toward the creature in the shadows. Ryuu saw the thing's eyes widen and began to move to avoid being hit, but it was too slow. The beam of light hit the creature straight in the face, and the darkness went away. Tarin growled and then turned his back to the forest. A blast of sound crashed over the clearing like roaring thunder. Dust curved up and split apart, tracing the path of the beam of light, making the leaves on the trees rustle about. Ryuu looked at his father in amazement. Whatever Tarin just did, it was so fast that it took everything else a few seconds to catch up with it.

"Are you all right, Ryuu?" asked Tarin brusquely.

Ryuu shook his head in confusion. "I...I don't know. I feel fine. What was that *thing*, and what did you just do?"

Tarin didn't answer him but crouched down and gestured for Ryuu to climb on. Only when Ryuu was on his back and they were in the air did he finally answer him. "That," he said, "was Lord Ivinrah I believe. So the nightmare returns as well."

Ryuu looked at him flabbergasted. "*That* was Ivinrah? Are you sure?"

Tarin nodded. "Yes, that was him. I can recognize those eyes anywhere. You were lucky that he was only able to destroy your sword and not you as well. It's unfortunate that he did that to Destiny, but you are still very lucky to still be alive. He could have crushed you."

"I can believe that," concluded Ryuu. "But what did you do?"

Tarin didn't answer.

"Father?" he inquired.

"Not now, Ryuu," was all Tarin would say. They flew in silence for several minutes; neither of them made a sound. During that time, Ryuu thought hard on what to ask his father next. He wanted to know so much, but he just couldn't decide what he wanted to learn first; it made his scar itch. He sat upright, inspired. How *did* he get his scar?

As if Tarin knew what he was thinking, he said, "Have you ever wondered why you have that scar?" Ryuu nodded. "Well, when dragons die, their spirits live on. Those souls search for the ones who are said to be chosen as the next generation of Dragon Knights. When they are found, the souls enter their bodies and live within them and merge themselves to the chosen one's soul, thus creating the scar on the chosen one's wrist. Each dragon had their own markings that symbolized their element. The diamond-shaped markings on my neck are an example of elemental symbols. Your scar has the same marking as mine."

"What are you saying, Father?" Ryuu interrupted. "You think a Twilight Dragon's spirit is inside me?"

Tarin laughed. "*Think?* I don't think. I know, and I know whose spirit it is."

Ryuu raised his eyebrows. "You do? Who?" Tarin swung his head around to look at him; a wide smile ran across his face.

"My brother's. Cyndrio's."

Ryuu gaped at him. "Your brother's? Are you sure?" Tarin chuckled deep in his throat. Ryuu almost took it as a growl at first.

With a sigh, Tarin answered him, "Quite sure." Then after a brief moment's hesitation, he added, "You have his voice."

Ryuu was speechless. He tried to speak, but words failed him. He then realized what his father was saying, and for the first time in his life, he was truly proud of who and what he was. He was honored that out of all the dragon spirits in the land, a Twilight Dragon's soul had chosen him to bond with. *Come to think of it,* thought Ryuu, still amazed, *my uncle's soul.* Not knowing what to say next, he stretched his limbs and yawned quietly and closed his eyes.

Just before he fell asleep, Tarin said to him, "When you wake up, we will be on the ground near the elves' capital, Synaigwa."

Ryuu sighed in acknowledgment and fell asleep, and once again he fell prey to his waking dreams.

When Ryuu woke, Tarin had spoken truly. They were no longer in the air but on the ground next to a stream in the elven forest.

"Where are we? Why have we stopped?" he asked as he slid off of Tarin's back. His knees buckled when his feet hit the ground, and he fell forward. Tarin swung his head around and caught him with his teeth and then lifted Ryuu up as a cat would a kitten.

"You need to stretch your legs for a while," said Tarin. "The lack of use has stiffened them up. Now the answer to your question. We're in the elven forest, Ashryno. We're about a mile away from their city Haidose. The others should be arriving here in another day or two. In the meantime, we should start traveling toward the elves' capital. They're expecting us."

Ryuu turned to his father, confused. "Now? We're not going to wait for the others to arrive first?"

Tarin shook his head and looked up toward the sky. "No, we have about twelve hundred miles to cover on our way to Synaigwa. By the time we arrive there, the others will arrive in Haidose."

Ryuu shook his head in protest. "No! I don't want to go to Synaigwa yet. I want to wait for the others first so we can go there together!"

Tarin swung his head back around and snapped his jaws an inch away from Ryuu's chest and growled. "I know you're worried about them! What makes you think that I'm not worried about them too? You and Christopher are the only family I have left, Ryuu!"

Ryuu bowed his head, ashamed. "I'm sorry, Father. I didn't know."

Tarin sighed and took a drink from the stream. Not knowing what to do or what to say, Ryuu stooped down by the stream and refilled his water-skin. Once it was full, he took a drink from the stream's cool flowing water. It tasted sweeter than the water he had from this morning. It tasted as if someone had just poured the remainder of their cider into the water.

"What's up with this water?" he asked Tarin, puzzled by its taste. "Why does it taste like cider?"

Tarin just shrugged, embarrassed, and took another gulp of the water. When he was finished, he said, "Strange things always happen around me. The flavor in the water is an example of these strange phenomena. I don't know how they happen. They just do. Sometimes the changes come directly from my feelings or thoughts."

"This has happened before?" interrupted Ryuu.

Tarin smiled. "Of course it has. Did you ever wonder why the Vera Tree was silver and gold? Or why Cyndrio Tower is so tall and wide? Or why the mountains around the tower are silver? Those things exist because of *me*."

Ryuu looked at his father, dumbfounded. "*You* made the tree that way? *You* built Cyndrio Tower? How?"

Tarin just shrugged. "I don't know. They just happened. You see, all the extraordinary things that I've done were for my family and loved ones in their honor of their passing."

Ryuu looked at him awestruck. Just how many amazing phenomena did his father achieve? Judging by Tarin's look, Ryuu had a strange guess that he knew what he was thinking.

"I'll tell you a few of my achievements on the way to the elven capital, all right?" said Tarin, smiling. Satisfied, Ryuu nodded and climbed onto his back again, and they took off and flew east toward Synaigwa.

THE ANCIENTS

Ashryno Forest passed below them as they flew to the capital. As Tarin flew overhead, Ryuu saw the creatures of the forest below. Occasionally, elven horned falcons would fly next to them. Unlike ordinary falcons, these falcons had two longer tail feathers and feathers above their eyes that curved up like horns. Tarin told Ryuu that all the creatures in the elven forest would be strange and unique to most creatures of their kind and that some of them could actually speak! He also told Ryuu about all of his achievements of the past: the Floating Crystal on the Toya Mountains in honor of his parents and his birth place; the gold and silver forest, known as Garindel Garden, in honor of his brother Garindel; the Silver Shrine in honor of Garindel's lover, Silva; the silver lake around Cyndrio Tower, known as Cyndria Lake, in honor of Cyndrio's lover, Cyndria; and the Vera Tree, in honor of his old lover Vera.

"Speaking of the Vera Tree," said Ryuu thoughtfully, "I saw the carvings on the trunk of the tree. It said something about 'my heart will always be pure for you.' I also saw the carving of the heart with your names in it, but there was something I couldn't read that was underneath it. Do you know what it said? Because I have a feeling that you do."

Tarin nodded and then said reluctantly, "I know what it says because I was the one who wrote it. It said, 'Here lies Vera, the one who loved me more than the world and even in my darkest hours.' And underneath that is a message from me that says, 'I love you, Vera, and honor you more than anything in the world, and I'm sorry for what I did to you.'"

"What language did you write that in?" asked Ryuu, unsure if he would get an answer. Tarin was silent for a very long time, and from the occasional jumping of his shoulders, Ryuu guessed that he was crying, or was it the flapping of his wing arms? He couldn't tell. It must have had been a long time since he had ever repeated those sorrowful words. Ryuu just realized how much Tarin had loved Vera. It made him question how much he loved Elizabeth.

"Father?" he asked, after another hour of silence. "What was the language you used on the tree, and what language was written on the blade of Destiny?"

Tarin said, "The language you speak of is the language of the Ancients. Christopher taught it to me when I was young. Now that I think of it, he taught it to me when I was ten."

"Who were the Ancients?" interrupted Ryuu.

Tarin cocked his head in thought and said, "I don't know very much about them, only that they were my ancestors. Christopher, who has always been different and stranger than everyone else, knows a great deal about them. He was born in the very place they were last seen before they went extinct."

"What's so strange about being born in Evelan?" he asked.

"Because," said Tarin, "Evelan was the Ancient's home and their capital. And there is another thing too. As soon as the Ancients vanished, the humans repopulated the area as if they were waiting for them to be no more, so I've been told. That all happened eighteen years before I was born, eleven years before the black meteor hit the Dark Temple to the northeast."

"What are you saying, Father?" asked Ryuu, thinking he already knew the answer.

"What I'm saying," said Tarin, "is that the Ancients didn't die out as it says in the old books. I believe they're still alive and that they are still living in Evelan as humans!"

Ryuu threw back his head and laughed. "Father, everyone knows they're dead and that they died out over three thousand years ago. What makes you so sure that you're right?"

Tarin turned his head around and looked at him scornfully. "Think about it. They were my ancestors. My very existence is a living memory of their powers. The Draggonians are also a living memory of what they once looked like. Ryuu, they were the ones who created Twilight Dragons because they were ones of twilight. The first Cyndrio came from them. Once they learned that Cyndrio had betrayed them, they used their power of twilight to protect themselves from him. Cyndrio knew he couldn't defeat them without help, so he tried to get other dragons to fight on his side, but they all refused to follow him, and they banished him to Darkensoan, the place where no one comes back alive, or so we thought."

"So he did return, but darker than before?" asked Ryuu. "And now that I think of it, it was the same day you met him, isn't it?"

Tarin shuddered underneath him and nodded.

"Did the Ancients play a part in his banishment?"

"Yes, they did. But back to what I was saying before. When the Ancients disappeared eleven years before I was born, it gave them seven years for their name to be forgotten from the peoples' minds. They did this as if they knew what was coming."

"The black meteor that brought Ivinrah?" inquired Ryuu.

"Exactly. They knew that the darkness was coming, and they didn't want to be found by the creature that was on it."

Ryuu nodded. "That makes sense. Maybe they are still alive. Yeah, maybe you are right."

Suddenly, Tarin lifted his head and began sniffing the air with his large nostrils, then wriggled with excitement.

"What is it?" Ryuu laughed.

"The elves!" exclaimed Tarin. "I can smell their cook fires! I can smell great roasts and rich spices. They must be expecting us!" With that, Tarin bellowed his excitement and started to slowly drift down to the elves.

ASHRONO VERAUK

As they entered a nearby clearing, Ryuu could finally smell all the wonderful smells Tarin kept jabbering excitedly about. As soon as they landed, the elves rushed up to greet them. *They are cheery people,* Ryuu thought. A lot more cheery than humans were, he had to admit. Eager to meet the elves for the first time, he slid off of his father's back to greet them. As soon as he did, he was immediately hugged and kissed on the lips by someone in the crowd.

"*Ryuu!* I've missed you," said the woman, and she buried her head in his chest.

"E-Elizabeth?" Ryuu looked down at the head buried in his chest; then his face brightened. "Elizabeth!" He hugged her tightly. "How did—"

"The wind was on our side," said another familiar voice.

Ryuu looked around and saw Kouri smiling at him and saw Melanie running up to him. Ryuu noticed that she took Kouri's hand, kissed him on the cheek, then whispered something into his ear that made him blush. Ryuu smiled at the two of them.

"Ryuu."

"Yes, Elizabeth?"

"There's someone here who you should meet."

"Who?" he asked.

Elizabeth giggled. "I want it to be a surprise."

Ryuu chuckled. "Well then," he said playfully, "let's see this person you want me to meet *so* badly." They walked along the crowd of elves with Tarin following behind them. Ryuu looked around for the others but couldn't find them among the elves.

"Where's Christopher? Where are the others?"

Elizabeth shrugged and said, "Well, Christopher said he wanted to meet someone, and the others are at the place we're going to."

Ryuu nodded and then asked, "So how did those two get together?" He jabbed his head over his shoulder in the direction of Kouri and Melanie.

Elizabeth turned her head to look at the two of them holding hands. She giggled. "He saved her life when we were ambushed on the fields as we were making our way to Evevana. He took on one of those black-cloaked creatures by himself when it tried to kill Melanie. But he was almost killed himself. The other knight with the ivory sword had to intervene to prevent the thing from harming him further."

"He looks better, then."

Elizabeth shook her head. "That's because you can't see the wounds. They're under his tunic. We haven't had time to tend to them because—" She cut herself off as if she couldn't bear to tell him.

Ryuu turned to her, concerned, his hands on her shoulders. "What happened?" he asked, hearing the fear in his own voice. What had happened to them when they were separated?

"Well... it's just that... No, you'll see for yourself. I don't think I handle saying it aloud."

"Say what aloud?" he asked, worried.

"You'll see. Come."

They walked through the elves' forest at a slow pace, taking in the scenery. The elves seemed to have taken their surroundings and built their homes to blend with the trees. Ryuu swore that he saw an elf open a door on a tree that didn't seem to be there and enter the tree. He looked up at the branches above him. He saw balconies that the elves had built into the trees, or was it that the branches just grew that way to look like that? He couldn't tell. On their way to wherever Elizabeth was taking them, Ryuu saw many of the elves walking about the forest path. They all wore robes like the ones he was wearing except that theirs were more colorful than his. They wore colors of emerald green, bright ivory, sky blue, terra cotta, ebony, gold, silver, maroon, and crimson. Most of them had bright yellow hair that shone in the sunlight. Ryuu blushed when a female elf smiled at him. She was so beautiful; it was hard to take your eyes off her.

"Hey!" said Elizabeth sharply, jabbing her elbow into his ribs. "Remember me?" Melanie had to laugh at that, for she was having the same problem with Kouri, who was gawking at the elven women. She jabbed him in the ribs too, but a lot more gently than Elizabeth did. *His injuries must still hurt him quite badly.*

The forest path seemed to go on for ages. Ryuu thought that they were lost until his foot touched stone pavement. He looked up at a beautiful stone archway with three giant stone statues of dragons (one above and one on each side). Each statue had two dragons (one male, one female), and they each shone bright silver. One of the dragons on the left looked a lot like his father.

"Wow," said Ryuu, bewildered.

"Wow indeed." agreed Elizabeth.

Then Ryuu was gently pushed aside. He didn't realize it was Tarin at first because he was in his human form. As if he was in a daze, Tarin walked up to the statue of the two dragons on the left. Without conscious thought, Ryuu went up to his father. Elizabeth gasped when she noticed how much the two of them looked alike.

"Ryuu, is this who I think it is?"

Ryuu turned his head around, and nodded. "Yes, Elizabeth. He's my father." She gasped a second time. Ryuu ignored this and asked his father, "Is this her? Is this Vera?"

Tarin nodded. He put out a hand to touch Vera's statue and stroked her face with the back of his hand. Distracted, he turned his head and gazed at something the others could not see.

He saw himself with his brothers, with Vera and her sisters, playing in the garden up ahead. Then one by one, the others disappeared, except him and Vera. They were alone and nuzzled each other happily and wrapped their necks together. Then Vera turned her head toward him and looked him straight in the eye as if she knew Tarin was looking at her. He smiled at her. She smiled back. Then she and his younger self faded away, like silver dust in the wind.

"Father?" asked Ryuu after a moment's hesitation. "Are you all right?" Tarin didn't answer. Ryuu was about to say something, but then a loud voice rang out.

"Tarin!" It was Christopher, and he was running up to Tarin. "Tarin! Come quickly. You are needed now!"

Seeing the panic in his eyes, Tarin went after him. Knowing what Christopher was talking about, Elizabeth and Melanie rushed after them, leaving Ryuu and Kouri at the archway.

Completely bewildered, Ryuu turned to Kouri and asked, "What's going on?"

"It's Cassea. She's dying."

"W-What happened?"

Kouri looked up at him and began to tell Ryuu what happened to them when he was gone, while they were traveling to Evevana. He told them how they were ambushed by the creatures in black cloaks, how one of them turned into a wolf and bit Cassea fiercely. "And then," he said, "Christopher became enraged when he saw that happening. I've never seen someone get so angry before; he took his Guardian sword off his back and began to brandish it like a wild man. The look on his face was more savage than the wolf's. When the wolf saw him, it ran for its life. When it was safe, Christopher picked up Cassea and carried her to the ship. You should have seen the fear in his eyes when he passed by, like he was remembering horrible distant memories."

He winced on the last word, clutching his chest. Ryuu put out a hand in case he should fall, but Kouri waved him away. "I'm fine." He winced.

"Are you sure?" insisted Ryuu. "Because that looks very much like fresh blood on your shirt."

Kouri looked down at his chest. He was right; the wounds had opened up again, and blood was pouring from them.

"I can heal that for you," offered Ryuu.

Kouri looked like he was about to refuse, then thought better of it and nodded. "All right, but can you help me remove my shirt? I don't think I should move too much." Ryuu nodded and began to help him.

Kouri turned out to be in more pain than Ryuu thought. Every time he tried to remove Kouri's shirt, Kouri would howl in agony. After the fifth attempt, Kouri fell against the archway, and Ryuu offered to cut the shirt open. Kouri agreed. By the time they got it off, the shirt was soaked and dripping with Kouri's blood, but that was not the worst of it! Kouri had three deep gashes in his chest (two side by side that ran down from the top of his right breast to the bottom of the left, and one that ran through the other two at an angle near his heart).

Ryuu looked away, revolted, and then forced himself to look back.

He placed his right hand over all three wounds and chanted, "Healria'oeso!" The wounds healed instantaneously, leaving nothing but three scars behind." That should do it," he said. "How do you feel now, Kouri?"

Kouri straightened himself upright and got to his feet. He took a few hesitant steps and then began walking around the garden behind the archway. Ryuu followed in case he should fall. With every step Kouri took, the more confident he became. After another minute of walking, he turned to Ryuu and announced, "Better. Much better. Come on. We should catch up to the others."

Ryuu nodded and then followed him out of the garden.

Ryuu could not help gazing at all the elves' stonework he saw. Beautifully carved statues of elves, dragons, unicorns, and draiphmores bounding about, carvings of the sea that led to their homeland, battle scenes from some war long ago, and, Ryuu was really amazed to see, a fifty-foot-long stone carving dedicated to the Twilight Dragons. These carvings were so detailed; Ryuu thought that they were alive. He was distracted when Kouri nudged him on the side and pointed to a stone building with people inside it.

They were about to head inside when Christopher came through the doorway. And in his hands was the body of a small girl. Ryuu looked down and paid his last respects. Cassea was dead. Christopher didn't even glance at the two of them when he passed by. Then a procession of elves followed Christopher in silence. Elizabeth spotted Ryuu and went over to him, tears in her eyes. She hugged him and buried her face against his chest. Then Ryuu heard the elves chanting a melody that touched the heart, that touched the soul. The melody was in elvish, but Ryuu knew the words and chanted with them as he cradled Elizabeth in his arms.

The elves continued to chant the song as they proceeded through the garden behind the archway. "What are they singing?" asked Elizabeth as they followed the elves.

"The *Ashrono Veŕauk*." Ryuu was surprised that Kouri was the one who answered. He smiled at him. He had forgotten that Kouri was brought up here as a child.

"W-What does that m-mean?" asked Melanie.

"It's their burial song," answered Ryuu. "They are singing about life and its sorrows." He also thought to himself that out of all the places in Cyndroania, this was the most peaceful place to die in, surrounded by nothing but nature.

They reached a clearing where elves from all over the forest were gathering. In the middle was a stone table, and on top of it was Cassea. She lay there as if she was only asleep. One by one, the elves stopped singing the Ashrono Veŕauk until one person was left singing its sorrowful verses. It was Christopher, and he was now singing in the common tongue. He sang thus:

"And may you find a darkness that trembles, and may you live and find your way. You do not see the path you've been chosen. You do not see how much I grieve. I walk this land without you at my side. If you do die, I'll no longer fly. Day lay oh day. We find our way. As darkness falls, I wander on. I fight along your side, your side, but I will not be there for you, and day will die, and I'll live on your side. I live to fight another day. Oh come to me, oh daughter of my friend. You may have died, but you're still alive. Give in to us. Be strong in your darkness. Head toward the light that leads the way. Be strong now. I don't want to see you die. Come to me. Oh come to me. Live on, live on, and live to see another day. You walk a road that no one can follow. You no longer need to hold on. Come now. They are calling. Come with me now and be at peace. Come to me. Oh come to me. I live on and die forever more. If you were not dead, I would sacrifice my life for yours and cry for mine. I live for you. I live for you. Oh come to me and be at peace!"

He finished his lamentation, and all was silent. Then Christopher bent over Cassea's form and kissed her on the brow. Then one by one, her family went up to her and paid their last respects; even Kouri paid his last respects to Cassea. When Elizabeth was finished with saying good-bye to Cassea for the last time, she hugged Ryuu and buried her face against his chest again.

This must end, thought Ryuu, anger boiling up inside him. *First Master Voggna and the peoples of Riverside and Oakwin, and now Cassea.* He bent his head to kiss Elizabeth on the brow and said to her, "This will end, but there are others that I need to find to help us end this coming war! For your safety, promise me that you will stay here with the elves while I'm away."

She hesitated and then nodded. "I will. For my safety and for my family's. But where will you go? And who will go with you?" she asked.

"No one. I'm going alone."

"Oh, no you're not!" said a rough voice. Tarin stood beside him and put a hand on his shoulder. "I'm not losing you again. And there's still much more that you need to learn before you are ready to fight against the enemy."

"He's right. I'm coming too," announced Kouri.

"And so will I!" This time it was Christopher. "The shadows fear my presence as much as Tarin's. You'll need all the help you can get, Ryuu. If you go alone, you'll die too."

Ryuu looked at them all, and his face brightened. Of course he needed help. Why should he go alone when he could have three other companions to fight by his side? He nodded to them and said, "Thank you."

His father chuckled, then said, "You will need more than your skills in magic and swordplay. No, you'll need a dragon of your own, to bond with it, and fulfill your destiny as a Dragon Knight of Cyndroania!"

"And you'll need the rest of us," said a voice from behind them. They turned around to find themselves facing two Draggonians. Ryuu recognized them at once. "Polpenrir? Sylrir? What are you doing here? I thought you two were looking for the chosen ones."

Polpenrir nodded. "Yes we are, but we came here to warn you about something that is of the utmost importance. We've found one of the chosen ones, but we barely managed to escape."

"Escape from what?"

"The Shadow Lords attacked us on the way here, but we manage to drive them off. Do you know about the two dragon eggs that you weren't suppose to worry about, Ryuu?"

"Yes, what about them?"

"Well, they hatched two days after you left for Riverside."

"They did? But, for who?"

"For me and Sylrir."

"That's good," said Christopher. "That means that two of the three most powerful dragons have hatched."

"What does that…" said Ryuu, but he was cut off by Sylrir, who said, "They are two of the four rarest kinds of dragons. Their magical elements are that of a special power greater than the original eight. The magical elements of the four most powerful dragons are Twilight, Nightfall, Dawn, and Shadow. I am the chosen one of Dawn, and my brother is the one of Nightfall."

Polpenrir nodded. "As I was saying. These two dragons hatched, and they grew rather quickly due to Koichi's spell that he placed upon them. He knew that the most powerful dragons needed to hatch first and grow faster than normal so they could use their full power against the Shadow Lords. My dragon, Kitsune, and Sylrir's dragon, Yoake, were the size of fully grown dragons and drove the Shadow Lords chasing us away."

Christopher nodded, pleased with what Polpenrir had told them. "Good. And the chosen one you mentioned? Which one is it?"

"Darkness," said Sylrir. "He was an assassin from Amrythilian, but he's not anymore. He knows what he truly needs to be now and why we brought him with us."

"Where is he then?" inquired Tarin.

"He was injured when we were trying to escape," said Polpenrir. "He's resting now."

"There's something else," interjected Sylrir. "As we were leaving Amrythilian, we saw black ships out at sea coming from the northeast."

Christopher's eyes widened at the news. "Are you sure that they were coming from northeast?"

Sylrir nodded. "Yes, I am. You know what this means, don't you?"

Christopher nodded. "I do. How long do you reckon it will take them to reach Amrythilian?"

"I believe," said Polpenrir, "they will be there by night fall. It's a new moon tonight. The Amrythilians will receive no warning I fear."

Ryuu looked at Christopher, trying to understand what on earth was going on. To Ryuu's surprise, he heard a voice in his head that said, *The black ships are from Darkensoan, the land of shadows.*

Rexon, is that you?

Yes, it's me Ryuu. Listen to what I'm about to tell. The Shadow Lords are sending their army of Shadow Knights to assist them with taking over Cyndroania forever!

But then, that must mean... But before he could finish his thought, Tarin spoke the words for him. "War is coming. We must warn as many people as possible when we're traveling tomorrow. I'll go tell the elven king what's about to happen so he can start preparing his people for battle."

Christopher nodded. "I think I'll come with you Tarin, there's someone I want to meet. It's been ages since we last spoke to each other. I wonder if she still remembers me?"

Tarin nodded in agreement, and they set off together. After a moment's hesitation, Polpenrir and Sylrir followed them.

"Ryuu," said Kouri, speaking for the first time since Polpenrir and Sylrir arrived.

"Yeah?"

"Lets go. The elves have prepared us a place to stay while we're here. Come with me. I'll show you."

And with that, they set off through the trees to a house that was made inside of one of the thickest trees. Ryuu looked up when they stepped inside the hollow tree. It had a staircase that was spiraled up along the inside wall of the tree trunk, leading to an upstairs bedroom.

"The elves said that this place was just built, and they're still working on it," said Kouri. "But they said until they can find us a more suitable place we can use the upstairs bedroom for tonight." Ryuu nodded appreciably, then climbed the stairs, and got into bed just as the sun was setting over the trees.

Ryuu had trouble sleeping that night. He continuously recounted all that had happened in such a short time, and he wondered what the future held. Who were the owners of the remaining dragon eggs? Would he gain enough of his own powers in time to stop the Shadow Lords and their armies? Would his dragon egg hatch soon? After many hours of turning these questions over in his mind, he finally fell asleep. And sleep was much needed as the road ahead of him was a long and treacherous one. And as he closed his eyes, miles away from where he was, the wailing and screaming of battle cries began to break the silence over Amrythilian.

The war had begun!